THE WITCHES OF THE CROSSWORLDS

BOOK I
SELLEMAE'S WRATH

The Witches of the Crossworlds
Book I
Sellemae's Wrath
Copyright © 2023 by Graham Anthony Davidson

ISBN: paperback 978-0-6459286-0-0
Second edition
First published 2017
Special thanks to all those who have contributed with their feedback
and support throughout the writing of these books.,

Published by Rack and Rune Publishing
rackandrune.com
email: info@rackandrune.com

For my children, Emily and Luke,
who taught me the meaning of fulfillment.

What People are saying about
The Witches of the Crossworlds: Sellemae's Wrath

CHAPTER 1

Patsy worried the crisp mountain air turning her breath to steam might give her away.

She should have been preparing for when her tutor would arrive, quizzing her about steam driven locomotives and all the other marvels of the modern age. Instead, the reluctant student stood peering around the corner of the house, watching the rickety sulky carry her parents away from the majestic manor and onto the road to Blackheath. Once it was out of sight, and the clatter of horses' hooves had faded into the distance, she stepped away from the house, turned, and skipped her way to the bottom of the garden, away from the housekeeper's ever-watchful eyes.

She sang to herself as she went, "Magpies and kookaburras..." Patsy loved singing; it was her favourite escape from the boredom of the rigid routine imposed by her parents.

It also helped her forget that her tutor, the cranky old widow, Mrs Bradshaw, was due to arrive at any moment.

The very thought of it made her anxious, especially after Mrs Bradshaw had lied so much to Patsy's parents by saying she'd been rude and insolent.

On reaching the bottom of the large yard, she looked over her shoulder and caught a glimpse of Mrs Bradshaw's carriage approaching the house. She took cover behind a shrub. Then, when one of the servants had taken Mrs Bradshaw inside, Patsy slid down the grassy slope and through the bushes leading to the dark world of the creek. Her father had warned her many times to stay away from its snake-infested banks, and Patsy knew she'd be in trouble for avoiding her lessons. But that mattered little as she picked herself up and ran down the creek to her favourite playground. Once there, she pretended not to hear the servants calling in the distance, and celebrated her escape by skipping stones where the creek opened into an expansive pool.

The servants' voices soon stopped as, one by one, they gave up, leaving the cicadas and a multitude of birds singing in the bushes as the only sounds around her, a kookaburra's laugh rising loud above it all. Patsy felt sure she'd be safe for now. She'd rather face her father's anger later in the day than spend the next six hours with a cranky old widow criticising everything she said or did. *Old widow...? More like an old witch*, she thought.

Patsy picked up another stone, crouching low as she drew her shoulder back and prepared to throw. Then something caught her attention. At first, she thought it might have been her imagination, or even one of the servants. But when Patsy focused on the sound, she heard it for what it was: a tiny voice pleading for help.

She called out in reply, careful not to be so loud as to be heard from the house. "Hello?"

There it was again: "Help!" Faint, but nevertheless, a voice.

"Where are you?"

The voice replied, "I'm near the big rock, across the other side of the pool. I'm stuck! Please, help me!"

Crossing would mean Patsy's dress and stockings would be soaked up to her waist, but she was already going to be in trouble, so what did that matter?

She slipped off her shoes and waded across the cold pool.

"Please, do hurry, Patricia!"

Patsy stopped. "How did you know my name?"

"I've known you since before you were born. I knew your mother, and your grandmother, when they were young girls… like you."

Patsy stood in the middle of the pool and folded her arms. There was something about this that didn't seem right. "You say you know my family, but I think you're lying. You're a stranger, and my mother has told me since I was little not to trust strangers."

"Oh Patricia, what can I do to convince you, to help you understand? I am no stranger. I am a fairy… the fairy who watches over you, and has watched the first-born daughters of your family for a hundred generations."

"Hmmph." Patsy wasn't convinced, but her curiosity compelled her to continue crossing the pool, her feet squishing in the mud at the water's edge when she reached the other side. A leech waved its head nearby in search of a host. Watching it for a moment, Patsy thought to herself that where there was one, there were always more, so she would have to be quick.

She leaned against the enormous rock, then twisted around to examine the dark space beyond. "This can't be!" Her jaw dropped, and she wondered if her mind might be playing tricks on her. There, stuck in an enormous and intricate web, was a beautiful fairy, no more than twenty centimetres high, with long slender limbs. A few centimetres from her right hand a small wand dangled, appearing ready to fall any second.

Despite the fairy's size, Patsy saw the relief in her eyes at the hope of rescue. "At last! Now please, Patricia, if you can just take my wand and place it in my hand, I'll be able to free myself. Then I'll grant you any wish your heart desires."

Patsy reached out to do as the fairy requested, then paused. She thought about what she'd read in some of the books on fairy tales in her parents' library. "How do I know you're a real fairy, and not some sort of evil pixie pretending to need help?"

"Excuse me, child? I don't quite understand."

"How do I know I can trust you?"

"I'm not sure I believe this! I could swear I just heard you express doubt. Are you serious? I'm a fairy! Come now, if you can't trust the fairy who watches over you, then who in this world can you trust? As I told you before, I've been watching over your family for countless generations! What more could you need to know? Please, you need to release me, or the spider will come and it will be too late!"

Patsy withdrew her arm, stood up straight and asked, "Why haven't you revealed yourself until now, when you suddenly need my help?"

The fairy let out a long sigh. "Oh Patricia, it's so very hard to come to terms with your doubts. Yes, I've worked hard to stay out of sight throughout your life, but it doesn't mean I haven't watched over you, as all good fairies should. We used to be happy to let children see us from time to time, but there's so few of us left now." She choked back tears. "Those of us who remain aren't prepared to risk being seen. I called for help only because I could see no other choice."

Her resolve softening, Patsy asked, "Why do you insist on calling me Patricia? I hate being called Patricia. You should know that if you've been watching so closely. Why can't you call me Patsy?"

"Oh, sweet, innocent child. We fairies are duty bound to respect the wishes of a child's mother in such matters. It would go against everything it means to be a fairy if I ignored such a fundamental understanding, one that has stood throughout the ages."

Patsy shook her head. "I don't know." She stood in the leech infested water, wondering how it would feel if she were the one stuck in that web. What if the fairy's nose became itchy, or even her foot? How frustrating would that be? "You'll grant me a wish? All I have to do is hand you your wand?"

"Whatever your heart desires, dear child."

Patsy hesitated, then thought of how much she'd love to have her old tutor back. Why did Miss Lawson have to go and get married, leaving her stuck with cranky old Mrs Bradshaw? Focusing on her wish, she leaned over and removed the fairy's wand from the web, taking great care as she placed it in the fairy's right hand.

The fairy gave Patsy a warm smile. "Thank you, sweet child."

The fairy swung her wrist and used the razor-sharp tip of her wand to free her right arm. In mere seconds, she'd cut away the rest of the threads holding her captive. "Oh, it feels so good to be free!" The fairy stretched her limbs, then flew about, circling Patsy's head before coming to rest on the rock. "I fear I'll need to rest awhile before I can fly off. My wings need time to recover from being so restricted within that horrid web."

Patsy looked smug. "Good, you'll have plenty of time then to grant my wish."

The fairy waved an arm dismissively and laughed. "Oh Patsy, you're hilarious! You actually believed the bit about granting a wish? Anything your heart desires? You need to accept reality!"

Already anxious about having to face the consequences of skipping her lessons, Patsy started breathing heavily. She clenched her fists and felt the pressure building in her temples.

But the fairy paid little attention to the danger brewing. "Why would I have been caught in that death trap if I could perform magic? You want to know what our wands are for? Do you ever grab a stick to cut down the spider webs in front of you when walking through the bushes early in the morning? Think about it, Pats. We're flying around all the time. Common sense has taught us we need to wave a stick in front of us as we go. The star at the top is only there to cut through the tougher threads, not weave some sort of magic. Ha! The only real magic I know of comes from drinking nectar, a bit too much magic sometimes. That's how I ended up getting—"

The fairy was cut off mid-sentence as Patsy snapped, picking her up and holding her tight around the waist. "You liar! You promised! You're just like that stupid Mrs Bradshaw! You treated me like an idiot and you lied to me!" She'd started shaking, and tears rolled down her cheeks as her grip on the fairy tightened. "And now, you're making fun of me. Why does everyone have to treat me like I don't matter?" Patsy stomped her foot as hard as she could, making a splash that spread high and wide. The action felt good, as if it was easing the pressure. "You lied to me… you promised me a wish. Why would you do that?"

Desperate to get away, the fairy stabbed her wand into Patsy's hand, triggering a reflex action. The girl cried out in pain as she flung her arm out and sent the fairy hurtling across the pool.

Trying to gain control of her flight, the fairy spread her wings, only to discover they were still too damaged from her time in the web to get her to safety. She hit a tree branch, then a rock, as she plummeted and fell headfirst into the water. "Help! I can't swim, help!"

Although still angry about being lied to, Patsy had no desire to see the fairy drown. She waded across to rescue the fairy once more.

"My wings, they're broken. I may never fly again."

Patsy took great care scooping the fairy out of the water. "That's okay, I can look after you while you get better. My father has plenty of glass jars in the garden shed. I'll keep you in one of those until you're ready to fly again. What do I need to feed you?"

Horrified at what lay ahead for her, the fairy replied with a single word: "Nectar."

A few minutes later, in her father's garden shed, Patsy hummed to herself while punching air holes in the lid of a jar, just big enough to hold the fairy. "I'll take you in through the kitchen. Cook likes to talk about fairy stories. So, can you imagine how amazed she'll be when she sees you?"

With her head slumped, Patsy's captive pleaded with the girl. "Oh, Patsy, please... I really don't think that's a good idea."

"Nonsense! Cook helped me care for a sick bird once."

"Did it survive?"

"No, but we wrapped it in a small cloth and kept it warm. We even managed to get it to drink a bit of water before it passed away. Cook's my favourite person in the whole world. Well, after my mother she is."

The fairy responded with an exasperated moan of anguish before falling silent.

Approaching the kitchen door at the back of the manor, Patsy's excitement was palpable. She burst through the door saying, "Look what I found, Cook! A real fairy!"

"Oh my God, child! Look at you! Covered in mud... and what are you doing bringing that thing into the house?"

Cook snatched the jar from Patsy. "Do you have any idea how worried we've all been about you? It took a good deal of convincing to get Mrs Bradshaw to wait for your return. I've no doubt she'll have cross words for you. You'd best take yourself upstairs, dry off and get into some fresh clothes so you can join her in the library."

"But, what about—"

"I'll not stand for any back-chatting."

•

As Patsy dragged her feet toward the stairs, Cook held up the jar and saw that three of the spider's legs had broken off. The poor creature was barely alive.

Ordinarily, she would have released it into the bushes outside, but on this occasion, she felt it would be cruel to release it when it would be so disadvantaged.

She took the lid off the jar, tipped the spider onto the pavement outside the kitchen door, and brought her foot down to end its misery.

CHAPTER 2

Dried off and wearing fresh clothes, Patsy made her way down the staircase. The household cat (a large ginger tom) greeted her halfway. Looking up at her, he let out a single meow. Patsy smiled, reached down, and picked him up. "Oh, Ferdinand, you're so lucky you don't have to worry about cranky old tutors." She could hear the cat purring as she continued down the stairs, holding him close so his face was next to hers.

Patsy stopped at the door to the library, Ferdinand's purr falling silent when he saw the old woman by the fire. He opened his claws and pushed against Patsy's chest, making it clear he wanted to get away. She let him go, then watched him race toward the kitchen. She wished she could join him, but because of her previous escapade, there would already be consequences when her parents returned.

Mrs Bradshaw closed her book and Patsy took a cautious step into the room. Her black dress, grey hair, and wrinkled flesh was just how Patsy imagined the witches in the fairy tales she'd read might look. After the surprise of seeing and rescuing an actual fairy earlier in the day, she knew they were real, so why not witches?

The widow turned to her, deep black eyes holding the girl in a vice-like grip. She spoke with a cold and flat voice. "Sit."

Patsy walked to the desk where the lessons took place. Her chair made a high-pitched scraping sound as she dragged it across the timber floor. Then, she took her seat in silence.

For at least a minute, maybe two, there wasn't a sound, other than the crackling of the fire. When the woman decided she was ready to speak, each word cut Patsy to the core. "*Never* has anyone treated me with such contempt." Another minute passed. "I want you to understand just how wretched you are to me. I want you to know how it feels to be so utterly rejected, the way you rejected me this morning."

Patsy took a breath, preparing to defend herself, then decided it would be safer to keep her thoughts to herself.

Mrs Bradshaw got to her feet and stared at the fire. "I have already called for the stablehands to ready my carriage." She turned to face Patsy and held up a key. "I will be locking the library door on my way out, and leaving the key with one of the servants. They already have strict instructions that the door remain locked until it is time for you to bathe and prepare for dinner."

Patsy's voice came out as a whisper. "But, I haven't had lunch, and I'm thirsty. I'll be stuck in here for hours."

"How is that my problem?"

As Mrs Bradshaw prepared to leave, Patsy could swear she saw the woman's shadow reach out and try to grab her with gnarled fingers. *That's another sign,* thought Patsy. *She must be a witch.*

Mrs Bradshaw walked from the room, turned, and closed the door. The sound of the key in the locking mechanism was the last connection Patsy would have with the woman for today.

What a relief that was!

Okay, she might be hungry and thirsty for a few hours, but she wouldn't have to face her tutor again for another week. Best of all, she had the library all to herself. It had always been off-limits to her unless she was having lessons or her father wanted to show her a specific book.

Now, for the first time ever, she could explore the library unsupervised. Without hesitation, she crossed the room to inspect her mother's writing desk. It was covered with intricate walnut inlays of strange symbols. The main one depicted three semi-circles, connected like links in a chain. Words, written in a language and alphabet she was unfamiliar with, followed the curves. She traced the symbol with her finger and remembered how Miss Lawson had told her such desks sometimes held secret compartments. She opened the cover, pulled out its myriad drawers to see what lay behind them, then started pressing against anything that stood out as a feature. She was about to give up when her hand brushed against a piece of trim on the right-hand-side of the desk. She slipped her hand under it and pushed up.

Click!

A door on the side popped open. She crouched down and looked in. A bunch of letters sat tied in a red ribbon, and next to them lay an ornate key.

Patsy pulled the bundle of letters out, sat cross-legged on the floor, and began untying the ribbon.

She clutched them to her chest on hearing the library door unlock, then reached into the compartment to grab the key. She stood facing the door, the letters and key hidden behind her back.

Relief swept over her when the door revealed Cook's rosy cheeks. "Shame on that woman, locking you in here without having had something to eat. I daresay Mister McIntyre will be looking for a new tutor when he learns of this. It's little wonder you hid from her this morning."

Patsy asked, "How's my fairy? Have you given her something to eat?"

"I'll not discuss that creature till I've got you fed, young miss. Come on now, I've a bowl of chicken soup and some bread for you in the kitchen."

"Can I take my writing book upstairs first?"

"If you must, but be quick about it, else your soup will get cold."

As Cook turned to leave, Patsy crossed the room, careful to keep the key and letters from any unseen eyes that might be watching. She opened her writing journal and shoved the bundle inside. Then, clenching her fist around the key and tucking the journal under her arm, she raced out of the library and up the stairs to her room.

Halfway up, Patsy stopped.

She'd left the secret compartment open!

There was nothing she could do now. She'd have to sneak back in after lunch to deal with it.

.

Patsy hid the letters and key under her pillow and made her way down to the kitchen.

She looked past the steaming bowl of soup on the table, instead focusing on the empty jar by the door. "My fairy! What happened to my fairy?"

Cook finished packing a stack of plates in the cupboard before she turned to the girl and replied, "Some things are best set free. It's cruel to keep a creature like that in a jar." She didn't have the heart to tell Patsy the truth of what she'd done.

"But it's not fair! I've never seen a fairy before. Now no one will believe me when I tell them how I rescued it from that horrible spider's web."

Cook remained silent.

"Will you at least promise not to tell people I'm lying?" Cook closed her eyes and chose her words carefully, then leaned across the table, looking Patsy in the eye. "I promise you, if anyone asks, I will tell them exactly what I saw."

Patsy smiled. "Thank you, Cook. Knowing that, I'm sure Father will believe me if you tell him too."

"I wouldn't be telling your father of it if I were you. He's sure to suspect you found it down by the creek, and you know how he feels about you going down there."

While Cook continued to get the kitchen in order, Patsy finished her soup then said, "I might go to my room now and have a rest. I'm frightfully tired."

"I'm not surprised after this morning's happenings. You'd best be quick about it if you really do want a rest, I'll be preparing your bath once I'm through here."

Patsy was starting to get up, then stopped and said, "Cook, I think Mrs Bradshaw might be a witch."

"Oh, and why might that be?"

"She's always cranky, and her skin's all spotty and wrinkled."

"Mrs Smith's old and wrinkled, do you think she's a witch too?"

"But that's different." Disappointed that Cook wouldn't agree, she got up, pushed her chair in, and made her way out of the kitchen toward the stairs. Once she was confident Cook couldn't see her, she diverted toward the library.

The door was locked!

Patsy backed away, then turned, ran up the stairs and into her room, closing the door behind her. She leaned against it while catching her breath, and wondered about what might be in the letters. And what about the key... what was that for?

Staring at her pillow, she crossed the room.

Who wrote them?

Who were they sent to?

She lifted the pillow, pulled out the bundle and sat on her bed, the letters resting on her lap as she untied the ribbon.

She lifted an envelope from the top of the pile, holding it up in both hands. Curiously, there was no address or postage mark, just a name, *Neridah*. It must have been either handed to her personally or slipped under her door, rather than sent through the post like most letters.

She pulled the pages from the envelope and began reading.

Thursday, April 4th, 1826
My Darling Neridah,

I cannot begin to tell you how happy I felt on receiving your reply.

It is now almost a year since you were widowed, and it filled my heart with joy last week when I watched from afar as young Meredith took her first steps.

Meredith? That was her mother's name! Neridah must be her grandmother... the one no one spoke of!

She continued reading.

Your father came to the stables again yesterday, lecturing my uncle about the importance of encouraging me to seek work in Parramatta or Sydney, saying I would find more opportunity in the city. Uncle Jeremiah knows him too well, and later confided to me his belief that your father merely wants me as far away from you as possible.

We are both adults now, and it is time we share what has always been in our hearts.

I'll wait for you before sunset this Sunday, at our special place down by the creek. Hopefully it hasn't been taken over by weeds in the years since we last met face to face.

Forever yours,
Alfred.

After years of asking about her grandmother, with no response from her parents, she was finally getting at least some answers.

She knew her grandmother's name! That, in and of itself, was a revelation.

And who was Alfred?

She grabbed another letter at random and opened it, leaving the first one open on the bed.

Saturday, June 21st, 1821
Neridah,

Since you taught me the art of listening to nature, life is full of surprises. Every walk through the bush is a revelation.

And you were so right about the cicadas and their gossip!

Far more wondrous though than any magic, or quirk of nature, was last week when first we kissed.

My life is forever changed.

I still think longingly of the first time we held hands, watching the pixies down by the creek. Since then, Bandah has become probably my closest friend, other than you of course.

Pixies? So, as well as fairies, there's pixies down by the creek? She tossed the letter aside and grabbed another, desperate to learn more.

Monday, December 1st, 1821
Neridah,

Why? Why must your father be this way? All because I lack the blood of the druids!

He tells my uncle to keep me away, and you run whenever I approach.

All because he heard of our love from one of the servants? I beg you, if our love means anything to you, meet me at sunrise by the creek. We can make our way to Blackheath and get a carriage to Sydney. We can start a new life.

Forever yours,
Alfred.

Patsy knew nothing of her great-grandfather's existence before now, but was already quite sure she didn't like him.

And again, she wondered… who was Alfred?

She was about to open another letter when there was a knock at the door, followed by the sound of the doorknob turning.

The letters on Patsy's lap fell to the floor, and she spread her arms in a futile attempt to shield the ones she'd tossed on the bed.

Patsy tried her best to appear calm, but her rapid, short breaths made the façade seem comical as she called out, "Who is it?"

The door swung open and Mrs Smith stepped into the room. "Nothing to worry about, Miss Patricia, it's only me." To Patsy, she appeared roughly the same age as Mrs Bradshaw, but with a larger frame and a thicker crop of hair. "Cook has started preparing your bath. I told her I'd come up to let you know it will be ready in the next half hour."

Mrs Smith was staring at the letters around Patsy's feet as she began backing out of the room. She stopped and said, "Oh, by the way, you might want to learn to cover your tracks in future. I've enough to do around here as it is."

"What do you mean?" said Patsy, trying to pretend there was nothing unusual about the letters.

"Suffice to say, it might be wise if you learn to close some things after you've opened them."

"Was that you who lock—"

She was cut off mid-sentence when Mrs Smith put a finger to her lips. "Shhh." The housekeeper left the room, pulling the door shut behind her.

Patsy fell back on the bed, a mixture of confusion and relief washing over her. Why had Mrs Smith said nothing of the letters?

At least now she knew who'd locked the library.

Once her heartbeat settled, she reached under the pillow and grabbed the key, examining it and imagining what it may open.

Was it for one of the old bookcases... the ones with the leadlight doors?

No, it looked too ornate for that.

But there were other things that had locks in the library, like desk drawers and cashboxes.

Yet it seemed too big to be used for any of those. Then, she remembered!

There was the big old book, the one on the wooden stand. It had a symbol on its front cover, like the one inlaid on her mother's desk, and it was held shut with an elaborate lock.

She'd asked her mother about it one day and had been told it was the old family bible... that Patsy's great-grandparents had lost the key when her mother was a baby. She explained how Patsy's father had wanted to pry open the lock, but relented when the Reverend Casey advised against it, proclaiming that to do so would be a violation of all that was sacred. Instead, he suggested my father should remain hopeful of one day finding the key.

Patsy lay there, rolling the key back and forth in her fingers. No point going downstairs to try it now, the door was locked.

But then, she had to go downstairs soon anyway for her bath, so why not go down now and check again, just in case? Maybe it was only locked while Mrs Smith was in there closing the secret compartment.

Her curiosity getting the better of her, Patsy collected the letters and hid them at the bottom of a drawer in her dresser. She opened her door and peered out to make sure no one was watching before tiptoeing down the corridor to the staircase. Hiding behind a banister, she was aware anyone looking up from below would likely see her anyway, but it gave her a vantage point where she could look down and see the door to the library. To her great surprise, the door was open!

She made her way down the stairs, clinging to the banisters as she went, and making a point to avoid the fifth step down, the one that always creaked when stepped on.

Darting from the base of the stairs to the library door, she made sure the room was empty before slipping through its grand cedar entrance.

There it was, at the far end of the room.

Patsy felt her heart would explode if it were to beat any harder as she approached the ornate book. It was covered in embossed green leather, with a brass inlay of the linked semi-circles in the middle. Each corner was adorned with a brass corner protector, and a large locking mechanism kept the book shut tight. She held up the key, debating the wisdom of what she was about to do. *Don't worry, Patsy,* she thought, *it probably won't fit anyway.* With a slow, deliberate movement, she slipped the key into the lock and tried turning it anti-clockwise.

Click!

She felt the pressure holding the book shut drop as the lock was released.

Unsure what to expect, she opened the cover and ran her fingers over the first page.

Even though the words and symbols looked meaningless to her, it was obvious as she turned the first few pages of vellum that this was no traditional bible.

A golden ribbon attached to the book's spine bookmarked a page in the middle. Patsy tried lifting the pages to get to it but was stopped when she heard voices approaching.

Her parents were home early!

Patsy shut the book as gently as possible, flipping the locking mechanism back over the cover. She fumbled with the key, panicking as she tried to withdraw it.

It was no good, the key was stuck!

With the voices now just outside the door, she dropped to the floor and crawled behind the desk normally used for her lessons.

CHAPTER 3

Colin McIntyre strode into the library, followed by Cook and his wife, Meredith. "How is it that she wasn't here when Mrs Bradshaw arrived in the first place?" His riding boots hammered on the floorboards as he made his way to the small table where he kept the decanters of rum and brandy, pouring himself a glass of the latter.

Meredith walked across the room, her petite frame appearing to glide as the hem of her long silken white gown hid her feet from view. Her face was framed by cascades of shimmering light brown hair that fell way past her shoulders.as she placed a gentle hand on Cook's shoulder. "Oh, Colin, you know what she's like. You can't expect Cook and the other servants to carry out their duties and know what our daughter's up to every second of the day. And if I had a tutor like that, I'd want to run away too."

"It was my understanding that part of what we pay them for is to do exactly that."

Cook's voice trembled as she stepped forward to defend herself. "Honestly, Mister McIntyre, sir, I never had this problem with her when Miss Lawson was her tutor."

Colin put the glass down and faced the servant. "And now you're suggesting I should dismiss her new tutor, who came highly recommended and at great expense, for teaching her the meaning of consequences?"

"She locked her in here without food or drink, sir. And then left for the day. If I can speak my mind, sir, I'd say she was being negligent."

"I'd call it discipline."

Meredith was quick to reply. "I don't care what you want to call it, I call it cruelty. I'm not prepared to stand here and accept someone treating our daughter that way, and neither should you. I know you want to protect her, and I love you for that, but in the process, you're far too hard on her at times."

Colin took a sip on his brandy. He knew there was no chance of him winning this battle, and that what Mrs Bradshaw had done was wrong. But damn that girl! Did she have to be so feisty? "Very well then, it seems I have little choice. I'll write Mrs Bradshaw a letter of termination in the morning." He looked toward Cook. "There was something else you wanted to tell me?"

"Yes, sir. When Miss Patricia returned from the creek, she'd taken one of your large jars from the garden shed and placed a spider in it. Biggest spider I've ever seen!"

"Go on."

"She insisted it was a fairy... honestly, sir, I worry at times about the imaginings that go on in that girl's head."

Colin and Meredith looked at each. After a small nod from his wife, he turned back to Cook and asked, "So, where is this spider now?"

"It's gone, dealt with it the same manner I always do with such creatures."

"Very well then, Cook, thank you for sharing your concerns."

"Am I free to finish preparing Miss Patricia's bath then?"

"Yes, please do."

"Thank you, sir."

Cook left the room as quickly as she could. Colin walked over to the fireplace, grabbed the poker, and used it to push the burning logs about until their dying flames sprang back to life.

"Colin, we need to tell her."

Colin bit hard on his lower lip. He'd secretly hoped Patsy would be able to go through her life without ever being burdened by the truth of who she was. "But she's still so young."

"She turns eleven next week; she's almost a young woman now. And if she's claiming to see fairies…"

"Yes, I know." He placed a reassuring hand on her shoulder. "Clearly, she has your gifts. The Reverend Casey is among our dinner guests tonight. I think we'd do well to seek his guidance."

"Yes, I agree."

"Speaking of dinner guests, I've matters to attend to in the stables. I'd best deal with them now, in case anyone arrives early and starts knocking at the door."

Meredith smiled, aware of what her husband was thinking. "Would you be thinking of the Danburys?"

"I like Charles, in small doses…"

Meredith placed a finger over his lips, "You busy yourself in the stables and do what you need to. I'll entertain the Danburys, and anyone else silly enough to arrive early."

"Thank you." Colin kissed her forehead, finished his drink, then made his way out of the library.

*

A spider? Cook thought my fairy was a spider? Patsy's foot became itchy, making it hard to focus. Beads of sweat dripped from her brow, and she struggled to keep her breathing slow enough to be silent.

On hearing her father's footsteps echo into the distance, she felt safe to relax a little and peer around the corner. Her mother stood in silence, surveying the room. *The key! Oh please, don't see the key.*

Meredith's eyes moved past the book, then locked on the desk where Patsy hid. Was that a frown on her mother's face? And if she could see her mother, didn't that mean her mother could see her? Patsy felt her lungs would burst if she had to hold her breath any longer. She didn't even dare blink.

After what seemed an eternity, her mother turned and left the room, pulling the door shut behind her.

Patsy felt giddy with relief. She walked over to the book and opened it at the bookmarked page, a folded note slipping out and falling to the floor. Patsy ignored the note as she stared in awe at the page in front of her. There, taking up almost the whole page, was an etching of a fairy, stuck in a web. The illustration was almost identical to what she'd been confronted with earlier in the day. On the opposing page was another image, this one depicting a gigantic spider, with human-like facial features, rearing up in front of an array of small cocoons suspended from the ceiling. Each one had an exposed head that appeared to be singing. Could that be the builder of the web behind the big rock? Surely not! Such a thing couldn't possibly be real.

She reached down and picked up the fallen note, unfolded the fragile page, and began reading.

I've little doubt the etchings on these pages convey the truth of my beloved daughter's fate.

Now my granddaughter, gripped by the bravado of adolescence, talks of crossing worlds to retrieve her. But I'll not let my only granddaughter sacrifice her own life in such a foolhardy endeavour.

I've ceased her training in the craft of our ancestors and will keep the Book of Wisdom closed to her from now on, along with her mother's journals, now safely concealed from her curiosity down where the gardeners keep their tools. Her training can only continue when she grows beyond such reckless ideas.

My heart would have me destroy this book, but to do so would be a sacrilege beyond imagining. So, I leave this note as a warning to any who may chance upon the key, or another method of opening its lock. Do not trust fairies lest you meet the same fate as befell my daughter.

CHAPTER 4

Patsy let her head sink down among the suds of the bathtub as Cook poured in another pitcher of hot water.

Cook's cheeks were bright red, and she shook her head while lecturing the young girl. "I swear child, you'll be leading me to an early grave with some of the mischief you get up to."

Patsy responded by sinking down further in the hope it would drown out the woman's words.

"I had little choice but to tell your parents about that creature you had in the jar, and they'll no doubt guess where you collected it from. Rest assured, when they catch up with you, you'll likely be in a world of trouble."

Thanks a lot, Patsy thought. *Does she have to remind me?*

Cook leaned over the bathtub to ensure she had the girl's attention.

"It troubles me that a girl your age should believe such a thing to be a fairy! You're far too old for such imaginings. I suspect your mother would be wanting to talk with the Reverend Casey about it. He knows a good deal about the workings of the mind and how it can be fixed through discipline and prayer. I've a good mind to have words with him myself."

Patsy raised her head from below the surface. "No! Please, promise you won't. You know the Reverend Casey scares me."

Cook's frown relaxed. "Don't worry yourself. I'll not tell a lie, should I be asked, but I won't be seeking to make trouble for you."

Patsy sighed and slid back down so her shoulders were submerged. "I don't understand why the creek has to be off limits. Father's happy for me to walk everywhere else on the property. He says it's because of the dangerous wildlife, but there are brown snakes and venomous spiders everywhere on the property."

"Shhh, child, you should know better than to question your father's wisdom. Now be quiet and soak for a bit. I need to go help Mrs Smith hang your washing. The poor woman struggles these days with her arthritis."

Patsy closed her eyes, humming as she slid further down in the tub. She hadn't realised she was drifting off to sleep until a sound from the corner of the room caught her attention, snapping her back to reality.

"Psst, Patricia."

She sat up and held her knees to her chest, shocked to discover she was not alone. "Who said that?"

"We need to talk."

Patsy surveyed the room; the only living thing she could see appeared to be a cockroach.

She glared at the bug and said, "That wasn't you I hope."

Rising from the floor to stand erect, the pixie put aside the shield he normally carried over his back for camouflage. He walked towards her and said, "There's no one else here as far as I can tell. But I digress. You created quite a problem this morning and we need to talk about it."

"Ugh! I don't believe this. I've had enough of creatures that aren't real for one day, so I'd appreciate it if you'd kindly disappear."

"Why do you doubt your own eyes? I saw you browsing through the Book of Wisdom. What you saw this morning was real. But more important are the forces you unwittingly unleashed." A dozen other pixies had entered the room, each carrying their own camouflage shield. "This is but a handful of the pixies who'll be gathering to protect you and your family tonight."

"Why? What do I need protection from? You're nothing but a cockroach that my imagination wants me to believe is something else. The fact is, you really are a cockroach, and when I've had a good sleep, I'll see you as such, and nothing more."

Although the Pixie's face was tiny, Patsy noticed his frown. "You'll think very differently by tomorrow morning."

"And why would that be?"

"The danger is coming, and it's worse than anything you could imagine."

Before Patsy had a chance to reply, the pixies raised their shields over their heads and went to ground. Cook's silhouette loomed large in the doorway. "Who's that you're talking to?"

"Oh, nobody, I was just—"

"Oh no! Cockroaches!" With her hands over her head to hold her courage in, the middle-aged woman rushed into the room, determined to stamp out the vermin.

Patsy protested, "No, Cook, no! They're really little people... like pixies. They were talking to me."

Cook froze. "Pixies you say? Talking to you?" The woman's eyes drifted skyward. "Honestly, Patricia, I love you dearly... your free spirit and your imagination... but it's getting too much. This morning you're telling me a spider is really a fairy, and now? Now you'd have me believe that cockroaches are pixies... and that they talk to you! Maybe it would be for the best if the Reverend Casey had a chat to you after all."

Cook was taken by surprise when Mrs Smith appeared behind her. "Oh, really Cook, I don't think that'll be necessary."

Cook replied, "I'm sorry, Mrs Smith, but is this really your concern?"

"I'd prefer it weren't, but the sun is getting low, and you'll be needed in the kitchen. I can get young Patricia dry and dressed."

Cook looked out the window at the sun just above the treeline. "Yes, I suppose you're right." She turned to Patsy. "It's your favourite tonight, and I will be putting turnips with it, so I expect you to eat them without complaint."

Patsy's eyes lit up. "Is it your special mutton pie? Please say it is."

"Aye, that it is. But Mrs Smith is right. Your parents will be having guests for dinner tonight, and there's much for me to be doing in the kitchen."

Once Cook had left, Mrs Smith grabbed a small stool and moved across to the tub. "Now, perhaps you might want to tell me about what you saw today... however strange it may have seemed."

The authority in the old woman's voice left Patsy feeling she had no choice but to comply. "Did you hear about the spider?"

"My understanding is that it was actually a fairy."

"What? Who told you? Was it Cook? Why would she do that?"

"You should understand by now that house staff don't keep secrets from one another, well, not about those things anyway. But trust me, I know far more about your day than Cook, or any of the other servants for that matter. The pixies warned me that the fairy was down there even before you rescued her, but it was too late by then for me to intervene."

"So, it really was a fairy… not a spider like Cook claimed it was?"

"It was both."

"I don't understand, how do you know so much about this anyway? Why would the pixies talk to you, and not the other servants?"

"Because I have been part of an ordeal almost identical to yours. It also involved your grandmother."

"You knew my grandmother?"

"I met her that very day. The outcome of her encounter with a fairy ended quite differently to yours. In her case, she unwittingly swapped her fate for that of the fairy in the web. She didn't know that every two score years, the fairies select one of their own to be left in the Spider Queen's web, so she can take it to sing in her choir."

Patsy said, "I saw the Spider Queen, and her choir. They were in the big book in the library. I'd thought they couldn't possibly be real."

Mrs Smith leaned forward so her face almost touched Patsy's. "Oh, she and her choir are real alright. She calls herself Sellemae. You helped her prize escape today, then hurt and imprisoned the poor dear before handing her over to an old fool who couldn't even see her for what she was." Mrs Smith grabbed Patsy's shoulders. "Listen to me! Sellemae will seek revenge, and it will be tonight. She'll seek to punish both you and Cook, then likely establish a nest in this manor."

Patsy pushed Mrs Smith's arms away from her. "No, I don't believe you! That's just something made up to scare people. It can't be real."

Taken aback, Mrs Smith replied, "With that attitude, it may be better that I don't tell you more of what's coming."

She held up a towel for Patsy to wrap around herself as she got out of the bath. "You need to dry off and get dressed. After dinner's done with, I'll be preparing you for what lies ahead."

"All I'll be preparing for after dinner is a good night's sleep."

"Trust me, you won't be getting much opportunity to sleep tonight."

Patsy set about drying herself off, then paused. Maybe, if she tried a more diplomatic approach, she might get some answers to help her work out what was real and what wasn't. She looked up at the housekeeper and said, "If you expect me to trust you, I'm going to need to know more about what's going on. I've been through quite a lot already today, and the more I think about it, the more some of what's happened just doesn't make sense." She paused again before continuing. "The fairy, the one I rescued today, it told me wands are just for cutting through webs."

"Aye, that she would. Anything to avoid honouring her deal with you. A wand is a powerful tool that can perform all manner of what you might call magic."

Patsy asked, "Why were you there when   my grandmother was tricked by the fairy?"

"There's no time—"

Patsy insisted, "I need to know."

Mrs Smith remained silent as Patsy finished rubbing herself down with the towel.

"It was you, wasn't it?"

"Enough of this useless chit-chat." She took the towel from Patsy and handed the girl her petticoat and dress. "You can get dressed and march straight to your room, young miss."

Patsy saw Mrs Smith's refusal to answer as an admission of guilt. She slipped into her clothing then asked, "What happened to her... what happened to my grandmother?"

Mrs Smith sneered as she moved closer and whispered in Patsy's ear, "I've no doubt your grandmother is alive, cocooned in Sellemae's lair… paralysed, yet conscious. She'll likely remain in that state for many thousands of years."

Patsy reeled back, struggling to keep her balance on hearing the revelation. "My grandmother's alive?"

Silence.

"Maybe there's some way we can rescue her!"

Patsy's attention was drawn to a small voice in the far corner. "Ha! Do you have any idea what that would entail?"

Mrs Smith turned to the pixie. "Don't you have something better to do?"

"She needs to know." The pixie flew toward Patsy then hovered in front of her. "The Queen's lair lies on a different plane of existence. It's barely possible to get there without being able to draw on the power of the Crossworlds… unless the portal opens."

"When will that happen?"

Mrs Smith replied, "Tonight, when the Spider Queen leads her army to seek vengeance on the foolish girl who stole her prize. Now, enough of this talk. There is much the pixie and I need to prepare."

The pixie added, "One thing you should be aware of, you will more than likely discover abilities—"

Mrs Smith cut him off, "Bandah! How is that helpful? She already knows more than she should."

"Bandah?" Patsy asked. "Are you the same… the one who knew Alfred? Tell me, who is Alfred? And what do you mean by abilities?"

Mrs Smith addressed Bandah. "Whatever abilities she may turn out to have, they won't be much help tonight, not on my reckoning."

Bandah replied, "I disagree. Sellemae is coming. Of all the perils in the Crossworlds, she is one of the most dangerous. We're going to need all the help we can muster if we're to see the morrow."

"You're not helping. Off with you, before I grab the fly swatter."

Patsy cried out, "No, I need to know more. Tell me, I need to know about these abilities, and about Alfred."

Bandah looked at Mrs Smith. She let out a sigh then said, "I can see I won't be rid of you till you've had your say. Go on then, get it over with."

Bandah returned his attention to Patsy. "Few people can see fairies for what they are. Those who can invariably have more capabilities. They easily learn to hear the natural world: the gossip of the cicadas, the poetry in magpie songs, and the sarcasm of kookaburras."

Patsy rolled her eyes. "But that's just silly. Cicadas talking? And magpies? They wouldn't even know what poetry is."

She jumped in surprise at the sound of a small, high-pitched male voice behind her. "Are you really so sure?"

She turned to see Ferdinand stepping out from the shadows. Hands on hips, Patsy stared at the cat. "Seriously? This must be a dream of some sort. I know for a fact that you can't talk."

Ferdinand casually sat and licked a paw before replying. "Oh? You might want to think about that."

"You never spoke before, why should you start now?"

"Have you ever bothered to listen?"

Bandah said, "Right now, you're hypersensitive, more able to free up your mind. You're hearing what nature is actually saying, rather than what you expect. Anyone can be taught to listen with practice, but for you, it comes naturally. You just needed a catalyst, like the events today by the pool."

"What else can I expect to discover?"

"I don't know. But one thing's clear, like your mother, and her mother before her, you're a genuine Witch of the Crossworlds."

This was getting ridiculous. None of this could possibly be real. And what gave him the right to call her a witch? "How dare you accuse me of such a thing!"

"Please, Patricia, you need to relax and hear me out."

She rolled her eyes again. "No, I don't believe I do. I know what I am, and I'm certainly not a witch, of this world or any other. I'll be turning eleven in a few weeks. So, stop telling me lies." Patsy's breathing grew short and shallow. She'd had enough of being treated like an idiot. Wanting to stamp out all the lies, she lifted her foot and brought it down hard, as though squashing an insect.

To the surprise of them all, Bandah went flying backwards, slamming hard against the wall.

Ferdinand asked, "Still doubt what the pixie has to say?"

"I've more than likely eaten something that doesn't agree with me. Like I said, none of this is real. It can't be!"

Mrs Smith assured her, "Oh, don't you worry, this is very real. There's little time left to prepare; the guests will be arriving soon. Once dinner's over, I fear events will unfold quickly."

"And what of my parents? Do they know about this? About this Spider Queen, or that I'm supposedly some sort of witch? And you still haven't told me about Alfred."

Mrs Smith frowned. "Enough of the questions, you'd do well to go to your room, NOW!" She leaned forward to add a touch of sarcasm as she continued. "And rest while you can."

"I don't want to."

"I don't recall saying you have a choice. If we're to protect you, you'll be doing as I say. I don't want to be having to tell your parents how you took those letters that you've got hidden in your dresser."

So that was why Mrs Smith hadn't mentioned the letters earlier. "That's blackmail!"

"Call it what you will. So long as it keeps you in your room till it's time for dinner. I'm not willing to run the risk of you getting up to your usual antics. There's too much at stake."

CHAPTER 5

Patsy marched up the stairs, with Mrs Smith close behind, while Ferdinand ran ahead.

When she entered her room, Mrs Smith remained outside in the corridor. "I'll collect you when it's time for dinner." She pulled the door shut, locked it, then walked away.

Patsy went straight to the dresser and looked for the letters. Seeing they were still there, along with the key, she made her way to the window.

Ferdinand jumped on the bed and set about getting comfortable. "That's twice in one day you've been locked in a room."

"Not for long." She opened the window as far as it would go and looked for a way she might climb down.

Ferdinand jumped on the windowsill. "Are you sure you want to do this? It's a long way down, you know."

Staring at the shed near the bottom of the garden, she replied, "I don't see that I have a choice."

She'd already swung one leg over the windowsill when Ferdinand said, "I wouldn't if I were you."

"Well, you're not me, are you?" Patsy lowered herself down so she was hanging by her hands on the outside, feet just short of the back veranda roof. She knew that if she let herself drop from here, it would make enough noise on the corrugated iron that any servants in the kitchen would be alerted to her latest escapade.

She moved one hand away from the windowsill and searched the sandstone wall for a fingerhold. Reaching out to her right, she found a small gap between the stone blocks, just big enough to work three of her fingers in as far as the first knuckle. It wouldn't support her for long, but should be enough for the second or so she'd need to lower herself to the roof. She gripped the sandstone as tight as she could, then eased her left hand away from the windowsill, not daring to breathe until she felt the roof under her feet.

Patsy sat on the roof with her back to the wall, looking for the safest spot to undertake the next stage of her escape. She could try to jump, but there'd be too great a risk of hurting herself. Looking to her left, she saw where the jasmine vine had spread from its lattice support and onto the roof. There was a risk her mother would be able to see her if she were in her drawing room, but it was a risk she had to take. She had to find those journals! It was her only hope of learning at least some of what was going on… from someone who wasn't going to tell her lies.

Patsy extended her feet toward the vine, then pushed with her hands to slide her backside along the iron, all the while being careful to stick to the parts where she could see it was nailed down. She hadn't gone far when the jagged end of a nail cut through both fabric and flesh. She resisted the urge to scream by gritting her teeth while silently counting to ten.

Once Patsy was within reach of the vine, the scent of the jasmine assaulted her nostrils, reminding her how it often gave her headaches and sneezing fits. *Not now,* she thought, *please... anything but that!* Conscious of an itch building in her nostrils, Patsy swung her legs over the edge and felt around with her feet until they'd found firm footholds.

She'd lowered her whole body from the roof onto the lattice when she sensed the sneeze coming. Closing her eyes, Patsy put a finger under her nose to block her nostrils, then held her jaw shut tight. She managed to reduce the sneeze to something that could barely be heard, then climbed down holding her now watery eyes shut to reduce the irritation, only opening them when she was past halfway.

Inside the drawing room, getting up from her chair and turning to face the window, was Patsy's mother. There was little choice but to jump, or her mother would see her for sure.

Patsy pushed away from the lattice, winding herself when she landed on her back. Confident she hadn't been seen, Patsy crawled behind the bushes until she reached a spot where she could make a run for the shed.

She sprinted away from the house, focusing on nothing but the shed and the cover it would provide. By the time she got there, Patsy was going so fast that she tripped while trying to stop, falling to her hands and knees in the muddy ground behind the small building.

She'd made it!

Looking toward the house to ensure no one was looking, Patsy slipped in through the door, pulling it shut behind her.

Where would someone hide a collection of journals?

She knew they wouldn't be in any of the drawers, but started by checking them anyway, rummaging around and taking out whatever was on top. She reached in with her hand to see if they were somehow concealed above the drawer, somehow wedged under the bench. Or, maybe they were concealed behind the drawers.

Next, she started checking the cupboards. She'd just opened the second cupboard when she heard one of the workers whistling as he approached the shed. Patsy rushed over to the door and pushed herself up against the wall, so as to be concealed by the door when it opened.

The gardener's voice boomed just outside the door. "I'm sure we'll get that one sorted before sunset Mister McIntyre, sir."

Her father was outside as well!

The door opened, and two sets of footsteps entered the shed. There was no mistaking the hammer of her father's boots on the floorboards as he entered the room. "I've no doubt a couple of good nails should hold it in place until we've cut some more timber to replace it."

Patsy held her breath, petrified of making the slightest sound.

The worker reached up to grab the jar of long nails from a shelf, then got distracted by the open cupboard and drawers not properly closed. "Begging your pardon, sir, but it looks like someone's been rummaging around in here."

"Yes, that would no doubt be my daughter. Cook mentioned earlier that she'd grabbed a jar and poked some holes in its lid this morning. I must have another talk to that girl about leaving things as she found them." Colin took a hammer from one of the drawers, then the two men left, pulling the door shut behind them.

Patsy let out a huge sigh of relief, then started checking the boxes stacked under the workbench.

Having searched the last of the boxes, Patsy sat on the floor, looking around and wondering where else they could be hidden. She tried to remember the words of the note… *where the gardeners keep their tools.*

The rafters!

There were more boxes stored in the rafters.

The heavy ladder swayed back and forth as Patsy tried to position it safely. Once in place, she clambered up its rungs then took careful steps along the wooden beams until she reached the two wooden chests. The hinges let out a loud creak as she lifted the lid open.

Empty!

She checked the second one, only to find the same result.

… where the gardeners keep their tools.

Patsy surveyed the room from her vantage point in the rafters, in case there was some possibility she'd missed. She looked at the assortment of shovels, rakes and hoes in the corner.

… where the gardeners keep their tools.

Where would she hide a collection of books she didn't want found? Certainly not in the places she'd looked so far.

… where the gardeners keep their tools.

There was nothing in the message that implicitly said they were inside.

Being on a slope, the shed had been built on piers. Could that be it? Could the journals be *underneath* the shed? The more she thought about it, the more Patsy felt sure that's where *she'd* hide them. She'd put them in a wooden box and wedge them under the floorboards, somewhere safe from the weather and where nobody would be likely to come across them.

Having made her way back down the ladder, Patsy looked through the window to check no one was watching, then slipped out the door and around to the back of the shed.

Choosing the spot where the clearance from the ground was greatest, Patsy crawled under, pausing to give her eyes time to adjust to the dim light before searching for a box that might contain books.

There it was-- two beams away and directly in front of her!

The slime and mud felt repulsive as she crawled across to retrieve the box, but once Patsy was back out in the daylight with her prize, she decided it was worth the effort.

She opened the box, lifted out the collection of books, then opened the first one to a random page.

Alfred asked me again today to explain how it is that I came to know the art of listening to nature and talking with animals. Oh, how much easier when all we shared was my lessons in mathematics, the sciences, and English.

Father says our language and what we learn from the Book of Wisdom is sacred, and must only be shared among druids and their bloodline.

But there are no druids in the Blue Mountains other than us, and I do so enjoy Alfred's company.

There are some things in life that mean so much more when shared.

Patsy turned to the next entry.

Today, I caved in. I don't care what my parents think, Alfred deserves to know the truth about my origins, and our ancestral oath to protect humanity from the perils lurking in the Crossworlds.

The perils of the Crossworlds. Wasn't that the term Bandah had used? She opened another of the journals at random.

I told Alfred the true extent of my powers this morning.
To say he was shocked would be an understatement...

She read through the page, realising that her grandmother really did see herself as a witch... a Witch of the Crossworlds. She turned the page and continued reading.

Today was my first experience, outside my dreams, of flying. After I'd snuck up behind Alfred and poked his ribs, he set upon chasing me through the bush. A tree had fallen across the path, and Alfred was sure to catch me if I stopped to clamber over it. Instead, I jumped as high I could, pushing the air aside with my arms, thereby pulling myself through the air. It's so easy to see air as nothing, but should you allow yourself to see it as one sees water, it's surprising how easily one can move through it... and the look on Alfred's face was priceless!

Still struggling to accept the idea she also possessed some manner of magical powers (despite what she'd already seen today, and her conversations with the pixie, Mrs Smith, and the cat), Patsy turned to a page further into the volume, hoping to find more conclusive evidence one way or the other.

It was my turn to be surprised today. A rare occurrence took place when a fairy appeared near the portal at the pool. The most amazing part was that Alfred could see her too!
The only explanation I can think of is that his ancestry

must link back to the druids as well! I can't wait to tell Father when he returns from Parramatta tomorrow.

Eager to learn of her great-grandfather's response, Patsy turned to the next entry.

Why must Father be this way? He says Alfred seeing the fairy meant nothing, other than that he is draining power from me, through a kind of osmosis … and that I should have nothing more to do with him.

I won't abide by his ruling.

I shall continue to see Alfred in secret.

She skipped a few pages and read on.

Father was cross with me again today, after he heard the cicadas singing to everyone that they'd seen me with Alfred by the creek.

Do they have to be so indiscreet? I know it's just their way of celebrating all that is good, but is there no way that two people in love can share time together in true privacy?

Meanwhile, Father continues to grow weaker. His powers have failed him, and his eyes have lost their sparkle. He says it's a sign that humanity no longer needs our protection.

Yet, my own powers grow stronger by the day, and Alfred managed to move a small rock today with the power of his will.

Aware she'd soon have to return to her room, Patsy flipped to another page.

I met the man today that I'm told I should marry.

Father no longer seems concerned with the need for me to wed a man with druid blood, but maintains his contempt toward Alfred.

My husband-to-be is the son of a wealthy squatter. He seems a good man, too good a man to tell the truth of what is in my heart, that it still lies with Alfred, and always will. I shall fulfil my duty. I shall marry him, and bear his children, accepting that to do so will mean leaving behind all I've learnt from the Book of Wisdom.

Patsy picked up another volume. It appeared on first inspection to be less used than the others. When she opened it, she could see why—there were just two entries.

Should I feel guilty? Am I somehow a lesser person for my failure to weep at my husband's funeral, and my inability to mourn him in the months since his passing?

I will always mourn the loss of a good man from this world, yet I still resent having been forced into marriage, and never once felt the connection a woman should toward her husband.

The only joy left in my life is baby Meredith's smiles and laughter.

I noticed Alfred watching from the stables today. Meredith took her first steps while we were in the garden enjoying the sunshine.

Oh, how I miss his arms around me and the tenderness of his lips on mine.

Patsy turned to the final entry.

> *Bandah finally told me the truth today, the real reason Father is on his deathbed, and why Alfred has developed powers of his own.*
>
> *It's not me that Alfred draws his power from, it's Father.*
>
> *The natural order has declared its hand, anointing Alfred to be my Father's successor as a protector of the Crossworlds.*
>
> *Bandah says the only way this process can be halted is for Alfred to leave. Tomorrow, when we meet by the creek, I will accept Alfred's offer to take Meredith and myself away from here.*
>
> *We will make our way to Sydney, where we will live as though married and start a new life together.*
>
> *Mother will then be able to use her knowledge from the Book of Wisdom to nurse Father back to health, while Alfred and I will be able to leave the burden of my druid heritage behind.*

If she wanted to piece the rest of the puzzle together, Patsy felt certain she'd need to learn more about Alfred.

The sound of a guest's carriage arriving reminded Patsy of the need to be back in her room by the time Mrs Smith came to collect her.

Patsy packed the books back in their box, and wedged it between the bearer and the floorboards once more. She kept low as she ran up the garden to the house, disturbing a pair of grazing wallabies on the way.

Having checked that no one was looking, she snuck into the laundry, confident it would be free of servants whilst so many preparations were underway in the kitchen. Patsy grabbed a sponge, wetting it so she could wash the mud from her hands and face, and grabbed a clothes peg before crawling past the bushes that lined the veranda. On reaching the lattice, she put the peg on her nose and climbed like a monkey.

A minute later, Patsy was back in her room. She removed the muddy dress and hid it under her bed, then collected a fresh one from her wardrobe. Ferdinand lay on her bed grooming himself. He paused to look up and ask, "Learn anything interesting?"

"I want to know who Alfred is."

"Oh, that tells me a lot. By the way, you might want to brush your hair before you go downstairs as well. We wouldn't want your parents believing the servants were sloppy about grooming you." Having said his piece, he went back to his own grooming.

Patsy looked in the mirror above her dresser. Her hair would have to do. She glared at the smug cat. The hard part wasn't so much getting used to the idea that he could talk, it was more about dealing with his attitude.

She'd just managed to get fresh stockings and shoes on when she heard the key turn in the bedroom door.

CHAPTER 6

Patsy took her seat at the table by the side of her mother, careful to ensure that nothing she said or did would embarrass her parents.

Colin sat at the head of the table, with Meredith to his right, and Charles Danbury on his left. *Damn it*, thought Colin. He was sure he'd instructed the servants to direct Charles and his wife to the other end of the table. Now, he was stuck with Charles getting in his ear about the virtues of moving to Bathurst and capitalising on the booming economies of the goldfields. "Can you imagine it, Colin? Between us, we could build the biggest hotel in the region. I've been told there's enough gold up there to keep the mines going for centuries…"

He'd heard it all before. Last week, Charles was extolling the very same virtues of Ballarat. And his grand ideas always hinged on Colin and Meredith selling their property.

There were a dozen or so guests for dinner tonight, a normal situation for a Friday. Among them was the Reverend Casey. Patsy couldn't help but notice how he glared at Mrs Smith as the old woman helped Cook serve out the entrée. She was taken aback when he turned his attention to her and asked, "So tell me, child, how was your day? Did anything out of the ordinary take place?"

Patsy recoiled in her chair. It was the first time in years the Reverend had even acknowledged her existence. "I had a very normal day, Your Reverence."

"Is that so? I wonder if the servants may have a different understanding of how your day was." He grabbed Cook by the arm as she passed the back of his chair. "Tell me, Cook, was there anything out of the ordinary that you may have observed?"

Cook's cheeks flushed bright red. She wanted to protect Patsy, but was aware of what a poor liar she was. "There was nothing of importance. Young Patricia found an injured spider in the garden, but it was of no great interest."

"A spider you say?" The Reverend turned to Patsy. "And where did you come across this 'spider,' my dear?"

The room went quiet, the guests feeling the urgency of the Reverend's questioning. Patsy looked to Mrs Smith for assurance, only to be dismayed when the woman ignored her. She was about to reply when her mother spoke up. "Spiders? Oh, come now, Reverend, do we really want to talk of such things at the dinner table?"

"There are many things in this world that are evil in their nature, and it is good to discuss them with the young. It can be the difference between them following an enlightened path or descending to a world of depravity."

Patsy's father took a sip on his wine then stood, his every word slow and deliberate. "Reverend Casey, you are here as a guest in my home for dinner this evening, and I will not have you talking to my wife and daughter in such a manner. Nor will I accept you manhandling my servants as you did just now with Cook. The only reason you've not been asked to leave already is that you are purportedly a man of God."

The Reverend pushed his plate forward, then stood himself. He was an imposing figure, despite his years, and taller than Patsy's father. His hands alone were almost as big as the plates they were eating off, and his balding head was framed by his long grey beard. "That being the case, I shall excuse myself. I have matters to attend to anyway." He stared accusingly at Mrs Smith. "I fear there are ungodly things happening in these parts, and I intend to deal with them as I must."

•

The Reverend Alfred Casey collected his hat and coat from the parlour, then walked out into crisp night air, feeling the occasional drop of rain. There would be a storm soon, of that he had little doubt.

As the priest approached his sulky, a cockroach flying by caught his attention. He reached out and snatched it from the air.

Bandah let out a strong protest. "Hey, there's no need for that! I was coming in to land anyway. What's your problem?"

"I'm not happy with the allegiance that's been forced on us, but I understand it's need. However, regarding what happened today… to be honest, I'd come to doubt that I'd see it again in this lifetime." He opened his fist, so the pixie could feel free to fly away if he wished.

Bandah put his shield to one side, lay back, and stretched before settling into the comfort of his friend's hand. He had a brief chuckle before replying. "Oh yeah, I totally agree. Allowing Mrs Smith to believe

I'd help her betray Patricia never sat well. But hey, we know what she's up to now, and it's exactly as you predicted. By the way, you did well in there. I could see that Mrs Smith was none the wiser about the charade you and Colin orchestrated."

The Reverend laughed. "That's doesn't surprise me in the slightest. She never was the brightest. I'm just glad Colin picked up on my signals. For someone making it up on the spot, the man was convincing."

"We need to make sure we're underway before she realises she's been conned. She plans to take the girl through the portal before Sellemae comes through, hoping to appease her by offering Patricia in place of the fairy. She's convinced herself that if she betrays me as well, Sellemae will restore her to her old fairy state."

"And no doubt string her up to spend eternity singing in her infernal choir."

"I don't think Mrs Smith cares about that. Her arthritis is a constant reminder of her mortality in human form. She'd prefer an eternity of servitude than face the reality of aging."

The Reverend shook his head. "She always was a fool. It's little wonder the fairies chose her as their offering." He climbed onto the sulky and set the horses in motion. "What of the girl? What does she know of what's going on?"

"She knows enough now that she may be useful in helping us pull this off. She's seen the book, and Neridah's journals. She's already found some of her power, and I believe she'll be formidable by the time she faces true danger."

The Reverend shook his head. "You're expecting too much of her. Formidable power without wisdom driving it will be our undoing. We must ensure she's relaxed and keep her protected. Once we've returned with Neridah, she can join her mother and grandmother in a trinity of power to close off the portal, and keep that vile creature in her own realm where she belongs. I'll park the sulky near the bridge, somewhere out of sight. Then we can work our way down the creek by the light of my lantern. We'll need to try to reach the pool before this storm breaks."

*

The mood in the dining room was sombre, punctuated by the sound of thunder from the approaching storm. Patsy watched on as one guest after another stood and made their apologies. With each flash of lightning, Patsy saw the departing guests' shadows appear on the wall as hideous creatures, leering at her with evil intent. Her mother took her hand. "Don't worry yourself, Patricia, it's just a storm. Although I fear it will be a big one."

Her father stood and addressed the departing guests. "While I understand the discomfort some of you may have felt over the Reverend's departure, I bid you please, stay till the storm has passed. I'd not want to see any of you get caught in the downpour and gale that's coming our way."

One of the departing guests replied for them all: "While we thank you for your concern, we all live within a half hour ride of here, and would like to ensure all is secure before the storm hits. Thank you so much for a wonderful meal as always." They were grateful the impending weather gave a cover for their early departure.

Within minutes, there was just Patsy, her parents, Cook and Mrs Smith remaining in the room. As Cook was preparing to leave the room with the barely touched plates of food, she was stopped in her tracks by the booming voice of Patsy's father. "Tell me, Cook, what exactly did you do with the spider my daughter showed you today."

This was the last thing Cook wanted. How could he ask such a thing in front of Patsy? "Begging your pardon, sir, but the creature was suffering. It needed to be put out of its misery."

"And she'd explained to you that it was actually a fairy?"

"Aye, sir, that she did, but I could see with my own—"

"Don't worry, Cook, you're not in trouble. Please, put the plates on the table and take a seat. There'll be plenty of time to clean up after we've finished discussing Patricia's spider. Mrs Smith, I'd be pleased if you could take a seat and join us as well."

The two servants looked to each other, then took adjacent seats, a few chairs away from the family.

Colin McIntyre chewed on a mouthful of mutton pie, then took a sip of wine. "I'm curious, Cook. Tell me, what else did Patricia tell you of her spider?"

"It was in one of your jars, sir, and she'd punched holes in the lid." Her lips were quivering as she continued. "She kept insisting all day it was a fairy, sir." She cast her eyes down as though she'd suffered a terrible defeat by having to betray Patsy.

"I'm pleased to know my daughter has such a vibrant imagination, and that my staff are capable of such sound judgements. Cook, I thank you for your honesty, and for preparing such a delicious meal this evening. It's sad so little has been eaten. You can feel free to return to cleaning up, but please, have the day off tomorrow. I'm sure we'll be able to hold the place together without you for at least one day."

"Thank you, sir! The market will be on in Blackheath, so I'll enjoy the chance to relax and walk among the stalls."

"Wonderful! I'll see to it that one of the stablehands drives you into town, and that he brings you home safely in the evening."

As Cook collected her stack of dishes and left the room, Colin

McIntyre turned his attention to his daughter. "I've told you before about going to the creek."

Patsy refused to look at him as she asked, "What makes you think that I got the spider from there? There's spiders everywhere around our property, especially in the stables and the laundry... even in your shed."

"Yes, there are. But this one, this one looked to you like it was a fairy."

"So?"

"There's only one place I've ever known of anywhere where spiders who look like fairies come from, and that's the large pool down at the creek."

Patsy's mother interjected, "Colin!"

"Something's going to happen tonight, Meredith. You and I both know it. The Reverend Casey knows it too. This may be our only chance to get your mother back."

Meredith's eyes betrayed her surprise. "Do you really think it's wise to talk of such things when Patricia knows so little?"

Mrs Smith replied, "It's not just wise, ma'am, but I believe it's now critical that you tell her all you can. She's already learned enough today that she needs to know some more. Your daughter has powers, and I believe they'll be beyond your own. You had little guidance to help you develop yours after your grandmother passed away. But today, young Patricia learned to listen to nature without so much as being taught the normal methods. Sellemae is angry about the theft of her offering, and intends to cross the worlds tonight and seek her vengeance on young Patricia and Cook for denying her the joy of another voice in her choir." She turned to Colin. "But you knew of this anyway, did you not?"

"Am I that transparent?"

"I've known you since you and the mistress were newborns. You can't hide anything from me, Colin McIntyre. No one else saw the signals that passed between the Reverend Casey and yourself, but they were clear as day to an old fairy like me. You seem to forget, I've lived for many thousands of years."

Patsy looked at her father and whispered, "It's all true." She turned and stared at Mrs Smith, then blurted out, "I knew it! I knew it was you!"

Colin looked at his daughter. "According to Mrs Smith, you've already shown you have powers. Do you have any understanding yet of what they may be?"

There was so much more Patsy wanted to say, but the words refused to come out. The uncomfortable pause in the conversation was broken by Ferdinand, who'd just taken his place on the chair across from Patsy. "Apart from talking to animals and using her anger to throw pixies around, she doesn't seem to know yet."

Patsy found her voice again as she watched her father listen to the cat. "So, you can hear him too?"

"Oh yes, your mother taught me how to listen years ago. There's a great deal I've learned from your mother."

Patsy turned to her mother. "Does that mean you're a witch too?"

Meredith was taken aback. She hadn't expected to face dealing with these issues so soon. "While I have some powers, I'm not one that should really be called a Witch of the Crossworlds, not like your grandmother. She learned from the Book of Wisdom, the big book in the library. But she was fooled, by a particularly nasty fairy."

Mrs Smith squirmed in her seat, wishing she could avoid having to respond. "You've no idea what I sacrificed that day."

"Oh, but I do… you've told me at least a hundred times a year since I first met you."

Mrs Smith opted to tell her again anyway. "As a fairy, I was immortal. Now, I feel the pain of arthritis and so much more. I'd lived thousands of years without aging before I became human. Now, in the mere space of forty years, I've been reduced to this."

Meredith was nonchalant. "Well, tonight, you have the chance to help us change the result of your deception."

"Oh yes, and how wonderful that will be. I'll extend my life by thousands of years, stuck with all the pain and aging I've endured as a human."

Meredith replied, "You should be more grateful, Mrs Smith. My grandmother took you in, and gave you a job as a servant, all thanks to the pleading of the Reverend Casey's uncle."

"Aye, that she did. And as gratitude, I did marry the man."

"Then led him to an early grave."

"It was the bottle that put him in the ground. And furthermore, I have to ask… who is it that benefits most from this arrangement? I can't help but feel your family has had the better part of it. I've worked tirelessly to protect your child from all manner of threats."

Colin McIntyre stood up. "Codswallop!"

Meredith reached across and touched his arm. "It's okay, Colin, we can deal with these details later."

"Oh, can we now? This storm that's coming, it's not natural. You know that as well as I do. There was just one thing I asked of you throughout these years, Mrs Smith, and that was to keep my daughter away from that pool. Of all days to relax your guard, you chose today?"

Mrs Smith's face contorted into a frown. "I find it so strange that you worked so hard to keep her from a place where you and the Mistress spent so much time together in childhood. Perhaps, if she'd been made more aware of what's down there, we wouldn't be facing this situation."

Ferdinand looked at Colin. "She has a point, you know."

"I didn't ask your opinion."

Ferdinand rolled his eyes and went back to grooming himself.

Throughout the exchange, Patricia felt she had little choice but to sit in silence. The fearful images of the guests' shadows as they'd left still disturbed her. As they swirled around in her head she whispered, "The shadows…"

Soft as her voice may have been, it still grabbed the room's attention. Her mother took her hand and asked, "What about them? Did they seem unusual?"

"When the guests were leaving, their shadows looked hideous, like the most horrible creatures. They resembled the demons the Reverend once showed me in one of his books. It was the same with Mrs Bradshaw earlier, her shadow even tried to reach out and grab me as she was leaving."

Meredith turned to her husband. "They're going after him!"

Colin replied, "Yes, and it would seem you were right about the need to look for a new tutor."

Patsy asked her mother, "Who are they? And who are they going after?"

"They are mind thieves, and if you've seen them, I've little doubt what their intentions are."

"What's a mind thief?"

Meredith took Patsy's hand in hers. "They're in league with the fairies. I've never seen one, and I obviously don't have that capability, or I'd also have seen them tonight."

Mrs Smith scoffed, "In league with the fairies? That's a good one! They were the ones who made the deal with Sellemae, promising to lure a fairy into her web every two score years, just as they did with me. They're no friends of mine, but that's indeed what she saw. I saw them too."

Colin's jaw dropped. "I don't believe this. You saw them, and you chose not to tell us?"

Mrs Smith chuckled as she replied, "Ha! Do you take me for that big a fool? My night will be so much easier if the Reverend doesn't make it to that pool."

Meredith said, "After all these years, and everything my family's done for you, you still care about no one but yourself."

Patsy groaned, "Ugh! You still haven't answered my question."

Colin stood up. "I'll have to go after him!"

Meredith tried to calm her husband, standing with him and placing a gentle hand on his shoulder, encouraging him to take his seat again. "Darling, there's nothing you can do against them now." She leaned closer and whispered, "Bandah is with him, at least we know he'll stand a chance."

Mrs Smith strained to listen in. If Meredith was trying to keep something from her, it could only mean one thing. "That infernal pixie! He's betrayed me!" She rose to her feet. "I must go after them, or this will never—"

She was cut off mid-sentence as she was flung against the wall. Patsy stood across the table, her arm pointing in Mrs Smith's direction. The old woman was at least a metre above ground level with her arms outstretched on the wall.

Patsy's breathing was heavy as she glared at the woman. "I asked a question and I want an answer. What's a mind thief?"

CHAPTER 7

Forty years prior, Alfred sat by the pool at sunrise, anxiously waiting in hope. He was almost ready to give up when Neridah came walking down the path, the early morning light glowing in her thick mane of red hair.

She walked up to him, reached up to place her hands on his broad shoulders, then ran her fingers down his arms till she took his hands in hers and leaned in to gently kiss his lips. "I'm coming with you." She rested her head on his chest. "I should never have listened to my father. Having been through a loveless marriage, I know now, more than ever, I want to be with you, and always have done."

"And what about your mother? Will she be okay, with your father on his deathbed?"

"I told her my intentions last night, and we have her blessing. She'll be bringing Meredith down to join us once she's had breakfast and dressed. Father doesn't respond to the herbs she gives him for the pain now, and even her most powerful healing methods do nothing for him. She says it's unlikely he'll even be aware of my absence."

Alfred held her, losing himself in the depth of her eyes. "You've made me happier today than I thought was possible. I've arranged everything. If we make our way to the Danburys', they've promised to give us a ride to Blackheath in their carriage. From there, we can get a coach to Sydney. My uncle has given me money from his savings to cover the fare, and enough for two weeks' lodgings."

"It's wonderful of Jeremiah to be so kind."

"He said it's to be a wedding gift. So, we'd best make sure we've taken our vows before we see him again. Bandah believes that once we leave, there's a chance of your father recovering. That his illness is due in large part to my presence draining him of the strength he draws from the Crossworlds."

Neridah shook her head. "I doubt that. He's been unhappy since the move from Ireland. It wasn't his desire to move here, but he felt compelled to follow the re-alignment of the portal. The climate doesn't agree with him, and Mother says he's been miserable since they first stepped off the boat from Ireland."

There was a long silence before Alfred said, "I saw a fairy down here one day. It must have been a year and a half ago, while you were still with child. She told me we'd be together one day."

Neridah put her arms around him and closed her eyes as she tightened her embrace. "Let's hope this is one occasion when a fairy actually tells the truth." Neridah eased her hold on him, lifting her head as though listening intently. She looked toward the rock on the far side of the pool. "Did you hear that?"

"What, the cicadas?"

"No, it sounded like a cry for help."

Listening closely, Alfred could hear it too: a faint distress call. "Help me please, I'm stuck in the Spider Queen's web."

The cicadas went silent, creating an eerie feeling around the pool.

Neridah stood up, pulled her dress up around her knees and entered the water. "Come on, Alfred, it sounds like a fairy. Let's see what her problem is."

Alfred removed his shoes, despite his misgivings. "Is this wise? Weren't you just questioning the trustworthiness of fairies?"

"Don't be silly, neither of us are fools." She continued making her way across the pool. "Trust me, we'll be alright."

Alfred waded in after her. "I'm really not liking this. Why'd the cicadas go quiet?"

Neridah stopped, then let out a groan. "Ugh! Will you please not be so boring? As well as having the strength of the Crossworlds behind us, we can both see and hear them for what they are. We've nothing to fear."

On reaching the other side, Neridah peered behind the large rock to see a fairy hopelessly tangled in a web, her right hand still gripping her wand, but unable to move. The fairy looked at her and breathed a sigh of relief. "Oh! Thank you for coming to my aid. If you can just touch the tip of my wand, it will draw enough power from the Crossworlds to set me free. But please be quick. I've been stuck here for ages, and I fear the Spider Queen is approaching as we speak."

Alfred was halfway across. "Neridah, please… don't be doing anything she tells you."

Neridah looked back. "Don't be silly, I'll be fine. It's just a fairy."

As she reached out to touch the wand, Bandah appeared from nowhere, trying to drag her hand away. "No! Don't do it! She's tricked you."

Neridah shook her hand, flinging away the pixie. She'd had a lifetime with her father telling her what to do. There was no way she was going to start her new life being ordered around by a pixie.

She touched the end of the wand and was immediately engulfed in a ball of shimmering light.

Alfred watched in horror as the light faded, revealing that Neridah and the fairy had exchanged places.

The fairy stuck in the web now bore Neridah's features and the young woman standing by the rock bore those of the fairy.

The woman who had been a fairy burst out laughing. "Yes! I'm free! Sellemae, Queen of all the Spiders, I offer you a wondrous tribute! Behold, I give unto you a Witch of the Crossworlds… in fairy-form. Come now and take her that she may decorate your lair." As Alfred looked on, Neridah faded away from sight, dissolving into nothingness within the web. The woman standing before him turned. "Now, I shall see to it that the witch's daughter is raised appropriately, that one day I may use her to return to the immortal fairy-state."

Alfred pointed an accusing finger. "Stay away from the child, or so help me—"

"So help you what? What's the matter? Lost for what to do without your little witch around to help?"

A voice calling from the opposite side of the bank interrupted them. It was Alfred's uncle, Jeremiah Smith. "Alfred! What are you doing? Who's that woman with you? Where's Neridah? I thought you'd be halfway to Blackheath by now."

Alfred had no idea how to explain what had just happened. When the woman turned to face Jeremiah, the man's jaw dropped. He couldn't remember having gazed on such a beautiful woman.

Two months later, the woman who'd once been a fairy married

Alfred's uncle, becoming Mrs Jeremiah Smith.

Stricken with grief, and unable to turn to his uncle any longer for support, Alfred sought counsel from the only friend he trusted. "I still can't accept this, Bandah. Surely, there must be some way to get her back."

"Not without the aid of a Crossworld Witch. Even then, it would be a journey fraught with danger. If you're going to attempt it, you'll need to spend a lifetime preparing for the hazardous trek into Sellemae's domain. I'll teach you all I can, but there is much you need to learn about yourself as well. You'll need to lead a life of discipline, so you can learn to focus your mind."

It was then that Alfred Casey made the decision to join the seminary and train as a priest.

*

The Reverend Alfred Casey heard a horse whinny from behind the bushes by the roadside. Eager to confirm his suspicions, he brought his sulky to a stop and dismounted. The light of his lantern revealed a path where tea trees had been flattened, leading to where Mrs Bradshaw's carriage and horses had been abandoned.

Bandah called out to him from the other side of the vehicle. "You might want to come around here and look at this too."

The driver was facedown beside it with a bloody rock next to his head. The Reverend Casey hadn't counted on Mrs Bradshaw being among those who would attempt to stop him. He now realised that he had less time than he'd anticipated. "It might be prudent if you fly ahead and see where the perpetrator may be. I'll continue on as planned, but if I'm to walk into an ambush, I'd like to know where it will be."

"I suspect whoever did this has been taken over by a mind thief. I've no doubt there'll be others who have been taken over nearby."

The Reverend climbed back onto his sulky as he replied, "I'd prefer you put your time into finding out rather than waste time speculating." He cracked his whip beside the horse and it took off. "I'll meet you downstream of the bridge."

He continued down the road till he reached a small bridge, its timbers rattling as he crossed. There was a clearing on the other side where he tied the horse to a hitching post.

As he crossed the road, the thunder of approaching hooves caused the Reverend to take a step back. A large riderless mare, that must have been at least seventeen hands at the shoulder, raced by, almost bowling him over when it passed within inches of him. As it disappeared into the dark night, he made his way down the bank and began wading through the icy water toward his date with destiny, a lantern in one hand and an ornate cane in the other.

A few minutes into his walk, he found Bandah waiting for him.

Bandah whispered in his ear, "The guests from the dinner tonight, all of them, they've been taken by the mind thieves. They're not much further downstream, and they've set themselves up on either side, lying in wait. Mrs Bradshaw seems to be leading them."

"Then I'd best make my way up the ridge and forge a path around them."

"No. That'd be far too risky. I've got a better plan."

CHAPTER 8

Mrs Smith struggled to breathe as she answered Patsy. "The mind thieves… they possess people. They go inside people's heads and make them do things. It wasn't Mrs Bradshaw who chose to lock you in the library earlier today. It was the mind thief controlling her." Satisfied with the answer, Patsy released Mrs Smith, letting her drop to the floor.

No one said a word as they watched Mrs Smith struggle to her feet, Meredith coming forward in a reflex action to help.

Then, a scream rang out from the kitchen.

Colin McIntyre raced out of the dining room, eager to find the cause. He froze when he reached the kitchen door.

He'd never seen so many spiders!

Cook was standing on a chair in the middle of it all, unable to take her hands away from her eyes.

Colin took a cautious step into the room. "Meredith, Patricia, you both need to come here right away." When Meredith and Patsy reached the door, Colin turned to his daughter and asked, "What do you see?"

"There must be at least a hundred."

"A hundred what?"

"Fairies, of course, don't you see them?"

Colin looked to his wife. "And what about you, darling? What do you see?"

"I see some fairies, but mostly spiders... lots and lots of spiders."

Brimming with confidence, Patsy entered the room. "Don't worry, Cook. I understand they may look like spiders to you, but they're really fairies, and I'm not scared of them."

One of the fairies turned to Patsy. "Well, you should be, especially after what you did to our sister. You couldn't have been more disrespectful if you tried."

Much to the fairy's surprise, Patsy ignored her, continuing to move forward. "I wasn't scared the first time I met a fairy, and I'm not scared now. Didn't you know? It turns out that, apparently, I'm a witch ... a Witch of the Crossworlds! And while I don't yet know exactly what I'm capable of, neither do you."

The fairies (or spiders, depending on where you were looking from) started to back away. "You can't protect her right through the night, witch. You'll soon be facing Sellemae in battle. This has been foretold!"

"I don't want to fight her."

"The great battle is already written in the future's history. Soon, the outcome will become clear to all as the words of the ancient texts come into focus."

Meredith stepped forward, putting her arm around Patsy's shoulder. "I've had enough of this! You fairies, spiders, or whatever you are. Your offerings achieve little more than to buy time from an evil creature to whom you owe nothing."

The lead fairy stood its ground as the others hastened their retreat. "It's not about debts, it's about respect."

Meredith replied, "Fairies know nothing of respect! Believe me when I promise you this, Cook will be safe tonight, because she'll be with us."

The fairy laughed. "I don't believe you people! Who are you to talk? You can't even see half of us for who we are. What an appalling way to go into a battle you're already certain to lose."

Ignoring the fairy, Meredith strode up to Cook and took her hand. "It's okay, Cook. Trust me, we'll keep you safe through the night."

Cook cried in loud sobs as she fell into Meredith's arms and watched the spiders dissipate.

•

The Reverend Alfred Casey took off his coat, as Bandah had suggested, and placed it on the creek bank next to his lantern. Hundreds of pixies silently flew in from the surrounding bushes, working their way through his coat and linking their limbs together as they went. Bit by bit, the coat began to fill out, until every gap was gone and it rose as a complete reconstruction of the man.

At first, the replicant swayed back and forth while the pixies grew accustomed to the coordination required to pull off their cunning scheme. Then, picking up the lantern, it made a gesture of farewell before heading downstream.

Just before reaching the area where the mind thieves lay waiting, the pixies diverted to a side trail, so as to take an alternate route along the ridge.

The Reverend watched from behind a bush as Mrs Bradshaw stepped out into the middle of the creek, holding a lantern of her own. "What a fool, believing he could outwit us." She looked up the hill at Alfred's lantern as the pixies carried it into the distance. "We'll split up." She pointed to the Danburys. "You two, go downstream to the pool, then climb up the ridge toward his light. The rest of you, come with me, and we'll pursue him from behind, cutting off the option of retreat." Without hesitation, they set off as directed.

Alfred waited until Mrs Bradshaw was well and truly out of sight and the sound of the Danburys splashing through the creek had faded into the distance. Although the mind thieves had fallen for the deception, they weren't likely to be fooled for long. But with luck, it would give him enough time to head downstream to where he could move through the Crossworlds without distraction.

This would be his first experience of crossing the thresholds between worlds since learning the secrets of how to do so from Bandah during his early days of training. He'd promised himself that he wouldn't cross between worlds until he was sure he had a chance to bring Neridah back with him.

Although the clouds from the approaching storm were closing in and a steady drizzle had started, there was still hope of finding his way by moonlight, but not for much longer.

He moved through the icy water, preparing himself mentally and reciting the mantra he'd been taught by his friend: "Umbah yimbah lundah, umbah yimbah lundah, umbah…"

After several minutes of walking, and bringing himself to the necessary state of mind, he came upon the area where the creek flattened out and expanded into a wide pool, the pool where Patsy had encountered her first fairy and the Reverend Casey had sat with Neridah as a young boy.

The Reverend could hear the Danburys scrambling up the ridge, but was unconcerned now about the consequences of being seen.

He pulled the handle out from his cane to reveal a long, slim sword. He held it over his heart as he continued the mantra, slowly fading away from this world and moving into another. A world dominated by darkness and chaos.

CHAPTER 9

Sellemae danced elegantly about her throne room, dangling her prize possession by a thread from the talon-like finger that extended from the end of one of her many limbs. "Oh, the joy! Yesterday I had but one witch, tonight I shall have, not just a second, but a third as well! What do you say to that, hmmm?"

Wrapped in a cocoon of silk with just her head exposed, Neridah ignored her.

"Oh, come now! That's so boring! After two score years hoping for the unlikely scenario where your lot may change, you still refuse to play by my rules?"

She stared down the queen, challenging her. "If your prize was taken from you, then my family's ready for whatever you may plan. My daughter will have had forty years to study and learn the craft. By now, her knowledge and power will be formidable. You have but one choice: you must accept defeat, before the battle begins."

Sellemae laughed, then turned to address the dozens of fairies in similar cocoons that hung by threads from the ceiling. She made a sweeping gesture with three of her limbs. "Sing a song of joy for me, my lovely guests."

The cocoon bound fairies burst into a beautiful melody that lit up the room with its sweet harmonies. The lyrics however, revealed a darker truth.

> *All hail the great Sellemae,*
> *May her evil reign forever stay.*
> *Her poison is so strong,*
> *We know to sing our song,*
> *Or else she'll make us pay.*
> *For when we do not play,*
> *She revels so in our fears,*
> *And loves to see our tears.*

The captive choir stopped when the doors to the chamber burst open. A contingent of the rogue fairies (fairies who voluntarily descended to the world of the Spider Queen in exchange for her granting them power to move more freely between the Crossworlds) entered the chamber.

Sellemae reared up, ready to strike. "How dare you barge in while I'm immersed in joyful preparations! Within the hour, I will open the gateway to the human world. Then I, the great Sellemae, shall avenge the theft of what was mine." She rolled all eight of her human-like eyes upward and continued, "What a sweet vengeance it will be! I shall take the witch and feast on the wretched human who squashed my prize underfoot. Then, I'll rid the manor they built so near my doorway of its vermin infestation. It will make a fine nest for my eggs. The human world shall become mine, as did this one... ten thousand years ago."

One of the rogue fairies stepped forward. "We know you've got these great plans for tonight, but we've heard news that may force you to make a few... alterations."

Sellemae swiped one of her eight arms at the rogue, only to be frustrated when the fairy flashed into a different world, coming back an instant later. "Grrr, you try my patience, fairy pest! Tell me, what is it that emboldens you to risk my wrath?"

"I meant no disrespect, Your Greatness, but I think you'll agree the matter is of great urgency. We received word the humans and the child-witch are preparing to descend to our world before we have the chance to rise into theirs."

"Ah, wonderful news! They'll save us the trouble of rounding them up in their world!"

"Be that as it may, there is more. The mind thieves told us the priest they've been warning us of also intends making the journey, aided by a horde of pixies. They're being led by a pestilent nuisance who calls himself Bandah."

"Interesting..." Sellemae brought several of her limbs around the rogue to embrace her. "You shall be richly rewarded for your dedicated service, and your recognition of the need to keep me informed." Her embrace became an ironclad grip. "However, I do not appreciate being interrupted during my entertainment! Do you dare to think such loathsome creatures could ever pose a threat to me in my own realm?"

The rogue tried to flash across to another crossworld once more, but found herself robbed of the ability to do so. Sellemae used two of her free limbs to wrap the fairy in silk.

"Your reward shall be rich indeed! One thousand years of service to my choir! Then you may understand the importance of leaving me in peace when I'm enthralled by the dulcet tones within the songs of praise to my greatness."

The rogue fairy was speechless as she was hoisted up to join the others in the void of the vast chamber.

Sellemae turned to the other rogues gathered by the door. "I will not have these pitiful creatures invade my realm! Saddle up the rats and summon the rest of the mind thieves. There can be no delay now in our departure."

*

The replicant of the Reverend Casey continued moving along the rugged track that ran up the hill, then down toward the creek again. The mind thieves began gaining ground, coming within a few metres of their prize just as its path forward was cut off by the Danburys.

Without warning, the pixies flew in different directions, letting the lantern and coat fall to the ground. In a moment, the 'human' form disintegrated. Within seconds, every pixie had crossed between worlds.

Realising they'd been fooled, the mind thieves released their captives, fleeing back to Sellemae's world. They hoped to warn her before she learned of the Reverend and the pixies from other sources.

Mrs Bradshaw and the dinner guests collapsed when the mind thieves departed. Men and women alike were exhausted, having been pushed beyond their physical capacity by their captors.

Their flesh and clothing torn, a sense of disbelief kept them silent. To make it worse, the lanterns had all gone out as the guests fell to the ground, and the storm clouds had covered the moon, leaving them in darkness.

They fumbled their way down the ridge in the darkness until they reached the relative safety of the pool. They looked up as one at the sound of Colin McIntyre's voice: "Who goes there?"

Charles Danbury, holding his tearful wife close, replied, "It's your dinner guests. Your somewhat traumatised dinner guests. What manner of poison did you dish up to us? We've all dined with you many times before, why do you choose now to show the kind of host you really are?"

Colin stepped forward, carrying his lantern. He had a flintlock in his other hand and a revolver holstered on his belt along with two large hunting knives. Close behind him were Meredith, Patsy and Cook. "I can assure you, Charles, what you've experienced has nothing to do with what you ate tonight and everything to do with forces you cannot hope to understand."

"I understand that my wife and I, along with your other guests, were unwillingly compelled to pursue the Reverend after you had rudely insulted a man of God at the dinner table."

Colin replied, "I've no time for dealing with your wounded pride. Tell us what you saw—what you remember."

Charles's wife, Lily, stood up, addressing her husband first, "What we've just been through? It's not his fault, nor his cook's." She turned to Colin and continued, "It was horrifying, as though we were taken over by demons. I remember everything, but as if in a dream. Whatever it was that controlled my body, I could hear its mind. We were following the tutor, Mrs Bradshaw, and chased what we thought to be the Reverend Casey, but it turned out to be something else. My captor vanished before I could understand what he thought it was, but I remember it cursing as it called out a name... Bandah."

"So, the Reverend Casey got away?"

"I believe so, but I learned more than that from the dreadful thing's thoughts. The one that they serve seeks to cause great harm to your daughter, and your cook. In fact, your whole family is in great danger, as I fear the rest of us are too."

Colin was distracted by the sound of splashing water downstream. He turned as a flash of lightning revealed Mrs Smith working her way through the far end of the pool, having used the nearby path. She was surrounded by what Colin saw as large spiders that appeared to run through mid-air.

Patsy looked across and exclaimed, "The fairies! They're helping Mrs Smith." She turned to her father. "We need to stop them!"

She was preparing to run over to them when Meredith grabbed the girl's shoulder and held her back. "It's okay, it'll be better for us if she's there anyway. If we wish to bring your grandmother back, she could be helpful in one way or another. She wants to trade places with her, even though it would mean an eternity of slavery. You see, she fears death. Fairies don't comprehend what it means to have a life like ours. They perceive it as too short to have meaning."

A crack of thunder followed another lightning flash, heralding the start of a downpour.

Colin had to yell as loud as he could to be heard above the rain. "Lily, I need you and Charles to take everyone back to the house. Feel free to help yourselves to warm blankets and a brandy if you wish. We'll see you back there soon and explain it all then."

The guests collected themselves together, relighting their lanterns to guide them along the path. A distant light from the McIntyre home became a beacon of hope as they struggled along.

Meredith asked Patsy, "Are you ready?"

"Yes, I think so."

Another lightning flash showed Mrs Smith and the fairies had disappeared.

Meredith nodded to her husband and they started wading into the pool. She looked back toward Cook. "Do you wish to join the others, or follow us as we cross over?"

Cook stood by the edge, refusing to budge. Her voice was barely audible against the background of the rain. "I'll fancy my chances better if I join the others at the house. I fear an unholy death waits for you if you go ahead with this." She turned and ran, wishing the Reverend Casey were at the house to offer some form of spiritual protection.

Patsy called out to her, a hint of panic in her voice, "Cook! Come back!"

"It's okay," said Meredith. "Cook will be safe there now Mrs Smith and the fairies have crossed over. Tonight's journey will be perilous, of that there's no doubt. Her fears of an untimely death are well founded."

They continued into the pool, the water now up to Patsy's knees. She looked up and asked her mother, "Do you fear death, Mother?"

"We all have to die sometime, and I've no desire to live my life captive to the fear of how and when that might be. So, no… I see nothing to fear in death. It's simply the thing that happens when life ends. What matters more than what might happen after death is that life itself isn't wasted."

When the water reached Patsy's waist, her father turned to his wife and daughter. "Okay, this should be deep enough. I think—"

Patsy interrupted, "No, we need to be closer to the rock! That's why the web's there, to be close to the centre of the portal."

Colin looked to his wife.

Meredith took his hand in hers. "We need to trust her instincts. They're stronger than mine."

Reluctantly, Colin moved in the direction of the rock, holding his firearms above his head to keep them dry.

A few metres from the rock, Patsy called out, "This is it, right here, I can feel it."

Meredith spoke, anxious to ensure Patsy understood the procedures they had to follow: "As witches, there are several ways we can cross between the worlds, but to take your father as well, there is just one. We need to encircle him with our arms and hold hands. Then, we need to close our eyes as we allow ourselves to be somewhere else. Do you understand? It's not about trying to be elsewhere, it's about letting it happen."

Patsy nodded and did as her mother asked… minus the closed eyes. She wanted to watch what was happening and couldn't see how some silly detail like having to close your eyes could be a problem.

As soon as she took her mother's hands, she felt the power. At first, it was like pins and needles circulating through their hands and lower arms. After a few more seconds, Patsy realised she could hear her mother's thoughts, even tap into her memory. A unique understanding ran through her mind as her mother's knowledge of witchcraft became her own. Then, she noticed the rain had changed direction, and was following with the flow of energy swirling around the three of them. The speed built up, and as it did, the water around them in the pool began following the rain. It built up until they were standing free of the water, surrounded by a swirling vortex. Patsy's eyelids dropped. There was nothing she could do to keep them open.

The next thing she knew, they were in darkness on a cold stone floor.

CHAPTER 10

As the Reverend Casey rose to his feet, a giant rat leapt at him. Without hesitation he thrust his sword toward it and the creature fell to the ground in front of him. A rogue fairy jumped off its back and hovered in the air before him.

"So, priest! Do you think your god can save you now? Do you think he'll be able to defeat the might of the great Sellemae?"

"My god doesn't need to lower himself to such tasks… not when he has me here to deal with scum like you!"

As the rogue lifted its wand to attack, the Reverend lowered his sword and extended the palm of his left hand toward the fairy. It hurtled backwards as a surge of energy from the priest's hand lit up the darkness, revealing what seemed an endless sea of approaching rats, some ridden by rogues, others by spiders.

The Reverend showed no hint of fear as he braced himself for the onslaught. He threw his sword javelin-style at the largest of the approaching beasts. His aim was true, bringing the creature's advance to an abrupt halt. At the same time, he swung his other hand across his chest, drawing strings of energy from multiple crossworlds to create an energy surge that forced dozens of rats to rear up and send their riders flying.

A spider the size of a large dog came within a metre of him and prepared its fangs to strike, only to feel them knocked away by the heel of the Reverend's foot striking hard.

The rats, wary now of the priest's power, held back as more spiders approached. The Reverend moved with the grace of a ballerina as he halted the advance of one wave after another, slowly working his way to his sword. He watched in horror when a mounted rat reached the spot where he'd crossed over and promptly faded away, travelling through the portal to the world of humanity.

Retrieving his sword, he swung it in broad arcs, sending broken spiders and their limbs flying in all directions. But he was unaware of a rogue fairy coming up behind him, close enough now to use its wand.

The rogue targeted him, preparing to send a surge of lightning-like energy toward the Reverend's heart. The first the priest knew of its impending attack was when he heard a gunshot ring out and turned to see the fairy drop to the ground dead.

Looking for the source of his salvation, he found the steely gaze of Colin McIntyre, a small puff of smoke rising from the barrel of his revolver. His face was lit by a glowing ball of energy Meredith was fashioning from the air in front of her. Patsy stood by her side, mimicking her mother's movements but having little success at creating her own light source.

As the dark army withdrew into the shadows, Colin stepped forward. "It seems our time of arrival was somewhat fortuitous."

The Reverend replied, "Aye, that it was. But let's not fool ourselves, our reprieve will be short-lived. We are greatly outnumbered, and they know it. Until Bandah and his pixies join us, I fear that, even with my power and that of your wife, we'll struggle to fight our way through this."

"I don't know about that. Don't underestimate what my daughter might be capable of." Colin approached the Reverend and placed a firm hand on his shoulder. "My apologies for my rudeness at the dinner table tonight, but I saw no other way of hastening our guests' departure so we could prepare. As soon as Meredith and I learnt of what was coming, it was clear we'd need to arrive here before Sellemae had the chance to cross over. I saw the mimicked conflict between us as the best way to create an excuse for you to make an early departure, while encouraging our other guests to leave as well. I thought we both managed to put on quite a show for them."

"No offense was taken, I can assure you. For my part, I was grateful that you recognised my need for a hasty exit. I suppose it would be appropriate to apologise for some of my choice of words as well. Even when used as a deliberate deception, such things can be hurtful. But the ruse served its purpose." He glanced at Patsy, then turned his eyes back to Colin and continued. "It's curious, McIntyre. Before today, it seemed unlikely your daughter had any powers at all."

"It appears they're triggered when she gets angry. After your departure, she lost her temper with Mrs Smith and effortlessly managed to hurl her against the wall of the dining room."

The Reverend raised an eyebrow then turned to Patsy, causing her to freeze under the weight of his gaze. "How are you coping, child?"

There's nothing to be afraid of, she thought. *He's here to help us.*

"I'm alright." Patsy took a step towards him. "I've always feared you in the past. I've heard you say such horrible things, both to me and others. But now I think that's all been a charade, like your argument with my father."

The Reverend Casey acknowledged her with a nod. "There are truths that are scarier than anything I've told you of. And I've no doubt we'll face many of them tonight. I'll be interested to learn more of what you're capable of when we do."

Meredith stepped forward, handing the glowing orb of energy to her daughter. "My power to use the craft became stronger the instant we crossed over. So much so, that this orb was almost effortless to create."

The Reverend Casey said, "That'll no doubt be because there are now the three generations in the one world: the Trinity of Power. Your mother told me often of the extraordinary access to strings of energy in the Crossworlds that would be accessible when three generations of Crossworld Witches come together."

Patsy looked up at the Reverend. "You're him, aren't you? You're Alfred!"

The Reverend Alfred Casey looked at her, but remained silent.

She stared into his eyes and saw the pain etched in his face, the forty years spent dedicated to the hope of one day finding the woman he loved. She said, "I've read your letters."

The Reverend cast his eyes down, as though they were dragged to the ground by his memories.

Seeing a need to change the subject, Meredith said, "I'm confident the orbs will last at least an hour. If we create a trail of them, it'll be simple to find our way back when the time comes to return home."

Colin shook his head. "No, we can't risk it. They'd merely give our foes a clearer target."

Patsy said, "Maybe we can still use them to help us." She rolled the orb in her hands, massaging it and stretching it as she teased and coaxed strings of energy through the countless layers of the Crossworlds. It grew and became brighter, to the point where it became difficult to look at. She released it and let it rise higher, continuing to grow as it went. The creatures of darkness surrounding them were uncomfortable in such light and backed away further as the illumination spread.

The Reverend glanced at Colin. "At least now we'll be able to see the foul beasts as they approach. Without darkness, there are few places for them to hide in this world. Tell me, Meredith, since your enhanced powers prove you've established a link with your mother, can you now sense the direction we must follow if we're to reach her?"

"I can only feel her ever so slightly. But if Patricia and I link hands, her location should become clearer."

Meredith looked deep into Patsy's eyes, taking the girl's hands in hers and once more feeling their instant connection and accentuation of power.

The power continued building within them, until Patsy felt compelled to release her grip. She stumbled for a moment, struggling to remain balanced. "I saw her!" She held a hand to her chest as she regained her breath. "I know where she's being held! We have to hurry, or we'll be too late!"

Without warning, Patsy prepared to run, stopped only by the Reverend Casey's strong hand locking on her shoulder in a vice-like grip. "Slow down, girl. We must consider our actions carefully, as each one could be our last. Our greatest danger tonight is the temptation to act in haste."

Colin McIntyre watched on as his daughter's frustration rose. She clenched her teeth, saying, "Let me go! My grandmother needs me!"

The Reverend Casey replied, "She needs us all, and she needs us alive."

Remembering her grandmother's journal entry where she described swimming through the air, Patsy flung her arms up, catching the Reverend Casey by surprise and breaking free of his grip. She jumped and pulled her hands back, lifting herself higher as she emptied her mind of all else and allowed it to be. Colin dived forward in a desperate attempt to stop her, managing to grab the heel of her shoe with his fingertips. Patsy kicked out, struggling to break away. "Let me go!" Another kick, and her foot slipped free of the shoe. She rose high above them, then looked down and said, "My grandmother needs me."

She turned to the east and headed off, travelling toward the distant palace of the Spider Queen. The others ran after her but struggled to keep up.

Realising there was no chance of catching her on foot, Meredith came to a stop. She pulled her muscles tight while reciting a mantra in the ancient tongue of the druids that roughly translated to, "Break these bonds and set me free, break these bonds and..." The fasteners on her formal dinner dress burst apart, allowing the gown to fall to the ground. Her modesty was protected only by the full length slip she wore underneath.

She closed her eyes, preparing to push herself into the air as her daughter had. *It's just like crossing between worlds,* she told herself. *Don't try, just let it happen.* She pushed up and left the ground.

To keep herself from falling, she found it necessary to keep her limbs moving, like treading water. Once she had the hang of it, a couple of frog kicks brought her close to Colin, albeit some distance above his head. "I'm going after her."

"We'll be right behind you." Colin and the Reverend did the best they could to follow from the ground as Meredith swam after Patsy, but they soon lost sight of her as well.

Seeing the two men were now more vulnerable without the witches by their side, the creatures of darkness were more prepared to brave the light cast by Patsy's energy orb.

As they ran, Colin hastily reloaded the revolver he'd fired earlier, then turned to the Reverend. "Now would be a good time for your pixie friends to make an appearance."

.

The fairies threw Mrs Smith to the chamber floor. The Spider Queen brought her face down to Mrs Smith's level. "So, the human that once was a fairy wishes to return to that which she once was. How quaint!" The old woman groaned as she struggled to lift herself enough to kneel in a sign of subservience. Grimacing at the arthritic pain in her knees, she tried composing herself, reaching out to the fang-tipped limb Sellemae extended to her. She drew the fang to her lips, kissed it and declared, "Oh great Sellemae, Spider Queen and rightful ruler of the Crossworlds, I come to you this day pledging eternal service in exchange for one small favour... that I may trade places once more with the witch you hold captive, and live an eternal life in your service as she withers away and dies."

Sellemae lifted Mrs Smith's chin with her fang, so she could look her in the eye. "You do appreciate the consequences of such a deal? That you shall carry the pain of old age through countless millennia?"

"Oh yes, Your Greatness. I am well aware of that. But I'd rather live in eternal pain than wither away and die in this pathetic form."

"Yes, but I prize so much having my witch, and it would be such a shame to watch her shrivel up and die while an old and decrepit crony like yourself lives on. You do see my point?"

"I also have information that may aid you in the capture of the other two witches invading your realm."

Sellemae flicked the fang of her extended limb, sending Mrs Smith to the floor with blood flowing from a deep gash on her brow. "How dare you suggest I may have need of your pitiful information to help me capture what has wilfully brought itself to me! You may be in human form, but you still think with the narcissistic delusion of a fairy! I'm always seeking new forms of entertainment, and tormenting you for a few thousand millennia does appeal to my sense of fun."

The Spider Queen reached up to the area where Neridah's cocoon hung. A fine strand of silk shot out from the tip of her talon-like fang, wrapping around the thread that held Neridah suspended from the ceiling. Sellemae pulled back and the line snapped. Mrs Smith gasped in shock as she watched Neridah's cocoon fall from the top of the dimly lit cavern. It seemed certain that Patsy's grandmother was about to hit the floor headfirst when Sellemae shot out another strand of silk, capturing her and pulling the cocoon to her feet. Her eyes stabbed at Mrs Smith as she turned to face her. "You will have your wish, fairy... but on my terms."

Sellemae slashed the cocoon open, lifting it slightly to spill its contents to the cavern floor, then gestured for the trembling Mrs Smith to take her place. She crawled toward the fairy-sized cocoon, still wearing her housekeeper's uniform, complete with apron.

Neridah lay there, still unable to move a muscle below her neck, as had been the case for many years. She looked up at the aging face of the woman who was once a fairy, the one responsible for her forty years of suffering. Was Mrs Smith seriously volunteering to reverse the spell, and as a consequence, experience countless millennia in this state?

It seemed she was.

The old woman extended a shaking finger to touch the tip of the wand that was firmly planted in Neridah's unmoving right hand. The spell reversal required desire on Neridah's part to trigger the transformation.

Nothing happened.

"Why should I?" asked Neridah.

"Why wouldn't you?" replied Mrs Smith. "Your daughter and granddaughter have crossed over. They wish to come and set you free. Your old boyfriend is with them."

"Alfred? Here? I don't believe you!"

"Reach out to them, feel them, and learn the truth for yourself."

Sellemae slapped a leg to the ground and laughed. "Hah! 'Your boyfriend is with them.' 'Reach out to them.' I so enjoy moments like these. If you can't convince her, then maybe I should string you up in front of her, so she can watch as you shrivel up and your bones crumble to dust." She looked at Neridah. "It would be a fitting and constant reminder of your lack of... dare I say it... humanity."

Neridah closed her eyes, unsure what to do. She knew Sellemae well enough to know she'd likely be freed from the fairy-sized cocoon, only to find herself strung up in a human-sized one. Then, she heard the distant call: it was her daughter and granddaughter, they were on their way! Not only that, but she could sense that her beloved Alfred really was with them. She looked up at Sellemae and said, "Okay, I'll do it."

Mrs Smith once again reached out and touched the wand, letting out a sigh of relief as energy surged through her veins. Yes! At last, she'd be free from the bane of humanity's pitifully short lifespan. The chamber was filled by a flash of light and the transformation was complete.

Sellemae picked up the limp Mrs Smith, once more in fairy form. "Foolish little fairy. You allow the witch to release herself and become what she was, and at the same time condemn yourself to such prolonged pain at my leisure."

"At least I won't die in the blink of an eye like those wretched humans and witches."

Neridah fell to the floor in shock, dressed in Mrs Smith's housekeeping garb. It was several sizes too large for her petite frame and hung loose on her shoulders. After four decades spent paralyzed below the neck, the sudden freedom of movement was like being reborn. The situation was still dire, but she had something that had been in short supply for throughout her years in captivity... hope.

And it was more than just the regained freedom of movement feeding that hope. Her daughter and granddaughter were here, creating a Trilogy of Power. Like Meredith, Neridah had never felt so powerful.

She sensed Patsy moving toward her at speed, and that she was closer than Meredith... close enough that she could reach out to the girl with her thoughts. Closing her eyes, she focused on what she wanted to tell her granddaughter. *I need you to be here. Release yourself from the restrictions of your senses. Don't come, just be here.*

In an instant, Patsy appeared, floating in mid-air above her grandmother as though treading water. Neridah explained as much as she could through their shared thoughts, desperate to share what she could while they had the chance. *Now we've established the Trinity, there are crossworlds you can move in and out of wherever and whenever you want... as long as the Trinity holds together. But beware, if you spend too long in another crossworld, the Trinity will be broken. I sense amazing power in you, and can feel through you that your mother has many gifts that she's yet to—*

Sellemae cut her off. "And all those gifts will be mine in but a few short minutes, along with the measly powers that you shall both no doubt try to use on me."

The Spider Queen lassoed Patsy and dragged her down. "You do know, don't you, that I can choose to draw your power out with my fangs? That is, if you choose to disobey me."

"Then why does my grandmother still have powers?"

Neridah spoke softly, "She has milked my powers many times, but there were not so many she could gain access to while I was in a fairy form. As time passes, the powers slowly restore themselves, allowing her to feed again and again."

Sellemae's laughter echoed through the chamber as she enveloped Neridah with two of her limbs. "And now, your grandchild can watch me drain all your powers before I consume hers."

Patsy's eyes narrowed as she got to her feet, still bound in Sellemae's silk. "Leave her alone!" She stamped a foot and the ground shook, surprising Sellemae so much that she loosened her grip on Neridah.

"Well, well, you are a feisty little witch! I'll have to find a very special place in my choir for your sweet young voice." Sellemae dragged Patsy closer. "Sing for me child, let me hear what qualities you will bring to the harmonies I so enjoy."

"I'll never sing for you, especially not after what you've done to my grandmother for all these years."

Sellemae lifted Patsy, dangling the girl before her eyes. "Oh, what a sadly misguided child you are. Have you not thought about the bigger picture? Look at how youthful your grandmother is. It's amazing, isn't it? I believe she looks younger than your mother. But that will change, when I drain her, not just of her powers, but of her life force! The choice is yours, little witch. Your grandmother's life, or my choir."

CHAPTER 11

O nce Cook had seen to everyone having food and blankets, she called aside two of the men. "We need to gather what we can to use against any spiders we might see—just the big ones mind you." As she spoke, a spider the size of a dinner plate raced toward her. Screaming in fright, Cook fell back, landing hard on her generous backside.

With Cook winded and unable to move, the spider leapt at her, only to be cut down as a hunting knife sliced through the air. The blade came to land next to Cook's hand, tip firmly wedged in the grain of the cedar floorboards.

The knife thrower was Vincent Donaldson, a wealthy squatter who enjoyed hunting. He addressed her as he walked up to take his knife. "I have to agree with you, Cook. The way this evening has panned out so far, the more protection we have, the better. We should make our way to the shed and collect whatever manner of shovels or pick-axes we can find." He helped Cook to her feet then retrieved his knife from the floor. "But we must stick together. We'll be safer in a group."

Everyone rose to their feet, most with blankets wrapped around themselves. The rain had just eased off and, as they made their way down the path towards the shed, Vincent felt the unnatural silence filling the garden. All the usual noises of the night—crickets, frogs and flying foxes—were curiously absent. Normally, after a storm like tonight's, the frogs would be deafening.

They had just about reached the shed when a loud screech broke the silence. Vincent looked over his shoulder then yelled to the others, "Quick, inside the shed."

Vincent's lantern cast just enough light to let him know he had no chance of evading the rodent bearing down on him.

The rat's weight almost crushed him as it pushed him to the ground. The beast opened its jaws, ready to bite, teeth scratching the side of his face as he drove his knife deep, bringing its attack to an abrupt end.

Vincent struggled to breathe under the weight of the dead rat. A large spider crawled off the rodent's back and approached his exposed face. The arachnid used one of its front legs to lift a lock of Vincent's hair from his eye, and the rogue fairy who appeared to Vincent as a spider allowed him to hear her voice. "Such bravery, yet so foolish. The question I have to ask myself is this, do I kill you or your friends first?" The spider's face was now a hand width from Vincent's. "The fun part of me wants the latter, but the—"

The spider's spiel was cut short by a garden fork coming down. The shock made her camouflage vanish for a brief moment, so she appeared as the rogue fairy she was, and a lucky one at that, the fork having pierced more clothing than flesh.

Cook lifted the fork and addressed what she saw as a struggling spider. "I've had about enough of you spiders… or fairies… or whatever you are. I've had it with being scared!" She lowered the fork to the ground and dispatched it the same way she'd dealt with Patsy's spider earlier in the day.

Cook turned to the dinner guests huddling inside the door of the shed. The rain started pouring down again as Cook called out, "Come on, we can't leave the poor man stuck under this foul beast."

Reluctantly, the guests came out, banding together to try and drag the rodent off their friend. They'd barely shifted it an inch when Charles was distracted by a glowing light coming from the direction of the pool. "I think we've got another problem."

*

The Reverend Alfred Casey looked across to Colin as they ran on. "We'll need to be wary of mind thieves as well. They're almost impossible to detect in our world, yet alone this one. If you feel a voice trying to enter your head, you must resist. Even if you're engrossed in fighting a battle, you must keep a part of yourself free to brace against them taking hold of your will."

Colin was distracted by the screech of a giant bat just metres from his head. In a reflex action, he raised his revolver and fired, bringing it crashing to the ground in front of him.

Turning as he ran, the Reverend pushed his palm toward another descending bat. Energy from dozens of crossworlds coalesced in his palm then shot out at their attacker, felling it as though it had been struck by a spear. More bats came at them. Colin had brought a good deal of ammunition with him, but unless he could find time to reload during the onslaught, it would be little help.

He could see at least a dozen bats overhead with hundreds of rats and giant spiders closing in around them, but had only five bullets still loaded in his revolver. "I hope you've got plenty of attack left in you, Alfred."

The Reverend pushed out another wave of energy drawn from the Crossworlds, bringing down an attacking bat. "I fear my strength will become exhausted by the time the rats are upon us, and I can bring down only one at a time with my sword."

Being careful to ensure no bullets were wasted, Colin waited till the next approaching bat was almost on top of them before firing. The bat's momentum kept it moving forward, making Colin leap aside to avoid being crushed. Rolling on the ground, he watched the Reverend send out energy pulses with both hands in quick succession as the winged primates converged on him.

A bat approaching the back of the Reverend's head was preparing to grab him with its razor-sharp claws. With no time to aim, Colin reached out and fired, hoping the bullet would hit its mark and not injure the Reverend by mistake. It tore through the bat's wing, causing only a brief pause in its attack, but giving enough time for the Reverend to bring his sword around in a sweeping action that sent the bat to its death.

Turning to Colin, he pushed his left hand forward, sending forth a burst of energy to cut down a giant spider that was preparing to plunge its fangs into the back of the man's neck.

More spiders approached, with the rats close behind. Colin brought down three of them in quick succession, then heard a dull click as he tried to fire an empty chamber. He stood up and grabbed the loaded flintlock from his back, swinging it like a club against three of the approaching arachnids, then aimed at the closest of the rats and fired, hitting his mark with deadly accuracy.

The Reverend's energy pulses grew weaker, until he had no choice but to rely on his reflexes and sword.

They were forced to climb atop a pile of the fallen vermin as they continued defending themselves. Colin slashed from side to side with the two hunting knives while the Reverend Alfred Casey was ready to resign himself to bringing down a few more creatures of darkness before being brought down themselves.

He slashed at a pair of rats, but failed to bring them down. He stabbed a second time at the first and grabbed the other by the fur on the back of its neck when, out of the corner of his eye, he saw a flicker of light in the distance.

Bandah and his horde of pixies had arrived.

*

Distress overran Meredith's mind, alerting her to Patsy's predicament. Instinctively, she emptied her mind of all distractions and allowed herself to be with her daughter.

The small flash of light that heralded her arrival in Sellemae's chamber distracted the Spider Queen.

Meredith wasted no time. She thrust her right hand forward, fingers extended toward the thread that held Patsy dangling before Sellemae's face. The energy surge was sharp and focused, snapping the thread and sending the girl crashing to the floor with a dull thud, still bound by the remaining silk.

The Spider Queen was outraged. "How dare you! You pathetic little witches dare to come into my domain, defiling the respect my loyal subjects feel toward me!" She slapped Meredith with one of her fang tipped limbs, sending her flying back onto the cold stone floor, her head hitting the ground so hard she blacked out.

Neridah raced to her side and cradled her daughter's head in her lap. It was the first time she'd seen her in forty years. "Oh Meredith, my sweet child. How beautiful you are."

"ENOUGH!" Sellemae stood towering over Neridah as she held her daughter. "It's time you experience the knowledge of real pain." Wearing a wide grin, she turned away and approached Patsy.

With no choice but to try escaping, Patsy staggered to her feet and tried to run, only to have her legs pulled from under her as Sellemae cast another thread and lassoed her ankles.

Neridah took a deep breath as she rose up, standing tall with her arms by her side. Closing her eyes, she took another breath, raising her now glowing hands high above her head. Her words were slow and deliberate. "Stay away from my granddaughter!"

Sellemae picked up Patsy and slung the girl over her shoulder, smirking as she faced Neridah. "Oh, and why would I do that? Who's intending to stop me? Would that be you?"

Neridah flung her arms at Sellemae, sending a bright surge of power toward the Spider Queen. Before it struck, Sellemae opened her mouth wide and let out a deep bellowing sound that wrapped itself around Neridah's energy surge, compressing and dissolving it as the sound wave pushed the energy into another crossworld.

Neridah, having put everything she could into the surge, swayed back and forth, struggling to remain conscious.

The last thing she saw before passing out was the Spider Queen laughing at the hopelessness of her attack.

CHAPTER 12

Much to the relief of Colin and the Reverend, the glow they saw proved to be more significant than Bandah had originally promised. There must have been tens of thousands of pixies.

Once positioned above the general area of the two men, they worked together to generate a blinding surge of light and heat, accompanied by an ear-piercing sound. Colin and the Reverend fell to the ground, struggling to protect their eyes and ears.

The reaction from the rats, bats and spiders was far more dramatic. Being used to a world of darkness, they reeled back in shock, giving squadrons of pixies the opportunity to swoop down on the attackers and prod them on pressure points, leaving them paralysed for several seconds, just long enough for the pixies to collectively raise the men above the fray of the battle.

They flew high, heading in the direction of the Spider Queen's palace, with bats constantly swirling around, unwilling to take on such a large horde of pixies.

Bandah hovered like a hummingbird before the Reverend's face as they moved along. "You look a little worse for wear and tear, my friend."

"Oh really? And why might you be saying that?"

Bandah laughed before replying, "It might have something to do with the tears in both your clothing and your flesh. In all honesty though, you two have done remarkably well."

"Aye, that may be so, but we looked certain to meet our maker before you finally arrived. Did you stop for supper before joining us? Or do you have a more rational explanation for the delay?"

"Come now, Alfred, surely you're capable of better than that. The moment you arrived here, there were pixies observing you from up high, way beyond the heights where these vermin could detect them. I've been traversing the Crossworlds, building as large an army as I could. Had we arrived even just a minute earlier, I fear our numbers would have been insufficient to snatch you from that rabble down there. Right now, though, you should rest, so you can recover while we carry you to your date with destiny."

Bandah was right. The Reverend looked at Colin McIntyre, admiring the way the man still looked so resolute and alert. But drawing the power from across worlds had left the Reverend exhausted. He took a long, deep breath, crossed himself, then recited a mantra he'd practised for decades in preparation for today: "Limbah yumbah, limbah yumbah…" Seconds later, he was in a trance-like state, in which each minute helped rejuvenate his powers far more than would happen through natural sleep.

*

Patsy decided she'd had enough. So what if she was bound in Sellemae's thread? She was angry, and she wasn't going to sit by and let an oversized arachnid hurt her mother and grandmother for one moment longer. "You'd better let us go," she demanded of the Spider Queen.

Sellemae took great joy in swinging Patsy before her eyes. "This should be good. Tell me, what are you going to do about it? Are you going to have a little tantrum?"

"You don't want to push me!"

"I wonder, should I be scared?"

Meredith had just started to come to, and panicked at the sight of Sellemae toying with her daughter. She took her mother's hand, sending energy through Neridah to make her aware of Patsy's dilemma. Neridah opened her eyes and squeezed tight on Meredith's hand. The two exchanged a glance, acknowledging they understood what to do.

The two witches thrust their free hands forward, summoning strings of energy from the Crossworlds that coalesced in a glowing ball. It floated before them, growing till it was three metres across. Then, with a gentle flick of their fingers, they sent it hurtling toward the Spider Queen.

Once again, Sellemae used a wave of sound to defend herself. But this time, she'd been caught unprepared, and was forced to drop Patsy in the process. She braced herself against the ball of energy as it broke through her sound wave (albeit with its power greatly diminished). Sellemae's head pulsed with pain when the energy ball struck. Neridah and Meredith worked to create a new ball, feeling they had the chance to take down their adversary.

But Sellemae was too quick for them. Just as they were about to unleash their next ball of energy, the witches' feet were dragged out from under them by one of Sellemae's web lassos. She dragged them across the chamber to be within striking distance. "You pitiful witches disgust me. How dare you defy me! Tell me, which one of you do I drain first. Oh, but wait, I don't really have to make that choice, I can drain you both together!" She raised her uppermost limbs high, aiming for the women's abdomens, and brought them down hard, only to have them come to an abrupt halt just centimetres from making contact. Frustrated, she raised them again for another attempt, but once more they stopped short of their targets.

Sellemae looked to where she'd left Patsy moments before. The girl was standing, her right arm extended toward her mother and grandmother.

She looked up at Sellemae. "I told you before, leave them alone!" She drew her hand back and made a sweeping motion toward the Spider Queen, sending the ball of energy, similar to that which the others had made, but with greater force than the previous one. Sellemae was unable to respond in time, feeling the full impact of the energy ball as it struck her in the face, sending her reeling back against the wall of the chamber.

Patsy raced up to Meredith and Neridah. The witches embraced, bringing the three generations together for the first time. Each felt an enormous surge of energy run through every inch of their veins.

Sellemae screamed in rage, "COME TO ME, LOYAL FRIENDS OF DARKNESS! Attack these vermin who dare to harm your queen. Make them understand what it means to feel fear!"

From out of the darkness, a multitude of glowing eyes came forth. There was all manner of creatures among the horde: rats, spiders, bats, and rogue fairies. Patsy could even sense the presence of mind thieves.

Sellemae regained her feet, and moved forward with her minions who were hurling spears and rocks at their targets.

The Trinity of Crossworld Witches, now telepathically linked, positioned themselves in an outward facing triangular stance. They shared each other's perception, enabling them to see everything around them. To conserve energy, they used the simplest powers at their disposal to divert the spears and rocks, making sure they fell short, or missed their targets entirely.

Working together, they emitted a glow that expanded outward as a protective dome. Whatever the forces of darkness threw at them simply bounced off.

Some of the creatures tried running through the glowing field of energy, but they too were repelled, receiving shocking burns as a reward for their efforts.

However, Semellae's army had numbers. They continued hurling themselves at the barrier, causing it to recede slightly with each hit. Semellae stabbed at it with multiple legs, shrinking it further with each blow.

Patsy shared a thought with her mother and grandmother: *I know how to beat her, but I can't do it while we're holding this shield.*

Meredith replied, *If we break this link, even for a moment, the barrier will collapse, and we'll be overwhelmed in seconds.*

Neridah disagreed. *If we don't do something soon, they'll be upon us anyway. We need to act while there's at least some distance between them and us. We need to trust in Patsy's power.*

CHAPTER 13

Colin looked at Bandah. "What's happening? Why have they stopped circling us?"

Bandah was also curious as to why the bats had changed course and were now heading toward the palace of the Spider Queen. "My guess is they've been summoned, which means your family must, at the very least, still be alive."

Colin asked, "Can't you fly any faster? At this pace, they'll get there long before us."

Bandah's annoyance was apparent, but he chose to remain silent. There seemed little point in explaining the obvious, that without the burden of ferrying Colin and the Reverend, the pixies would have arrived at their destination long ago.

An uncomfortable silence accompanied them for the following few minutes of their flight, only broken when the Reverend Alfred Casey emerged from his meditative state. He brought his head upright and opened his eyes. Bandah asked, "How do you feel?"

"I'm ready."

Bandah called out to the rest of the horde, "Okay, time for the crossworld jump. The three generations of Crossworld Witches are together, so we'll be able to find them more easily. That, and the strength of the Reverend's power will be enough to take Mister McIntyre with us when we allow ourselves to be with his family." He moved toward Colin and confessed, "I couldn't let you know we could do this jump until Alfred was ready. Sorry if you find that disturbing."

"I'll get over it, one day."

Bandah called out, "Okay, let's do this!"

A few seconds later, pixies began disappearing. Initially, it seemed at random, but Colin was sure he saw a pattern emerge as the pace of the disappearances increased.

The wave of vanishings swept up Colin and the Reverend, sending them headlong into the middle of Sellemae's chamber, directly above the Trinity of Crossworld Witches, but outside the remains of their protective shield.

For the first time in forty years, Neridah and the Reverend made eye contact, albeit for the briefest of moments. Yet within that moment, they conveyed all the hope and love they'd ever felt for each other, and the realisation that to hold each other, they would have to survive a battle with the odds stacked against them.

It gave the Reverend a renewed sense of purpose.

He let out a yell of defiance, throwing himself clear of the pixies and landing among the advancing beasts. He pushed out with his hands and made a sweeping action as he hit the ground, energy surges flowing forth from each palm. The creatures of darkness were sent tumbling back, as though caught in the raging current of a flooded river. Sellemae was preparing to bring a fang tipped limb down on the Reverend when Colin fired his flintlock, hitting one of her eyes. It distracted her enough for the Reverend to see the threat and evade the claw-like fang.

The Spider Queen was outraged. "You! The lowest of all the pitiful creatures in my realm tonight… you dare to throw your firecrackers at me? I'll enjoy watching my babies feed on your flesh!"

Colin replied by pulling out his revolver and firing bullet after bullet at the Spider Queen.

Sellemae laughed as she absorbed each of them. When the revolver's chamber had emptied, she moved closer. "Now, puny human, prepare to meet a painful end!"

She stabbed with one of her forward limbs, aiming for the centre of Colin's chest. It was stopped short, a pillar of metal having appeared from nowhere, with Sellemae's fang-like claw embedded deep within it. She struggled to remove it, but the pillar was anchored in many more crossworlds than this one. "Which of you vermin is responsible for this? I DEMAND TO KNOW!"

Patsy stepped forward. "No one calls my dad puny!"

Sellemae cast a web toward Patsy, only to have it dissolve as soon as it touched her. Another metal pillar materialised, encasing the end of the limb she'd just employed. "What is this? How dare you! Know this, girl, my vengeance is like nothing you can comprehend. Release me now, or pay the price."

"I'm not scared of fairies, and I'm not scared of you." Patsy focused hard, bringing forth power from several thousand crossworlds. She focused on the harmony of the dancing strings of energy, each threading its way through all the known crossworlds. She summoned them to herself and used her will to pull them through into the one crossworld… the crossworld of the Spider Queen. They instantly coalesced and solidified, transforming into six additional super-dense pillars, each holding captive another of Sellemae's limbs.

Patsy then looked to the approaching creatures of darkness. "Anyone wish to challenge me?"

The creatures began backing away while Sellemae screamed, "Come back you cowards!" She turned her gaze to Patsy and prepared to hit her with a sound wave, only to be thwarted by an energy surge that took her by surprise.

It had come from Meredith.

With Sellemae reeling and barely conscious, Meredith raced forward and embraced her daughter. "Oh, my darling! I'm so glad you made it through."

Patsy smiled and fell into her mother's arms.

The Reverend Alfred Casey approached Neridah. Tears formed in his eyes, blurring his vision so much he had to wipe them away to see her clearly. "You've not aged a day."

"Under the circumstances, I suppose that's to be expected. But Alfred, I'm astonished. You waited for me? For all these years?"

"Aye, that and more. I've dedicated my life to preparing for this night. I never gave up hope of bringing you home."

Neridah looked at his torn body and saw the strength he'd built through constant training. She looked at his face, saw the grey of his hair, the beard and the etched lines that seemed an apt counter for the years. Lastly, she looked deep into his eyes, and the years became meaningless. In them, she saw his innocence, commitment, determination, and his heart of gold. But most of all, she saw his love for her. Tears streaming down her cheeks, Neridah draped her arms over his shoulders and pressed her cheek to his chest.

Patsy walked up to the Spider Queen and placed her hands on her hips. "I'm going to leave you like this in the belief your minions will look after your needs until the power holding you in place fades. By then, I'll have made sure you'll never be able to find your way to my world again."

"Ha! You know nothing of magic or the power you possess!"

Patsy looked toward her mother and grandmother, then back to Sellemae. "Maybe not, but I know one thing. I couldn't hope for better teachers." She took in a deep breath, then thrust a hand toward the spider, sending a powerful surge toward her face. Sellemae's head went limp as she lost consciousness.

Colin stepped forward, a sense of urgency in his tone. "We need to leave."

He was surprised to hear a voice from among the cocoons suspended above them. It was Mrs Smith, sounding distant due her reduced size. "Please, don't leave me here. I don't deserve this!"

Colin spat out his response, "You deserve everything that's coming to you."

Patsy was horrified. "No Father! How could you even think such a thing! No one deserves this! We should free them all, whatever they may or may not have done."

Bandah landed on Colin's shoulder. "She's right you know, there's no avoiding it. Before we leave, each and every one of those cocoons needs to be cut open."

Colin sighed as he looked away. He thought about it for a moment then replied, "It would appear I have little choice in the matter, other than to accept the dictates of my daughter and a pixie."

Meredith said, "Whatever we do, we need to be quick about it. I doubt those creatures of darkness are just retreating, I think they're heading for the portal."

The Reverend replied, "I agree, we'd best cut these fairies down and be on our way." He turned to Colin. "With some help from Bandah and his crew, you and I can deal with this. Your family should head back now to defend your home. We can join them once we're done releasing this choir."

Neridah grabbed his arm, her fingernails digging deep. "No! Surely, there must be some other way. Why must we be separated again? I'll stay, and—"

Alfred placed a gentle hand on her shoulder and put a finger to her lips. "No, you three are only safe against those hordes for as long as you stay together. It'll take us little time to set these fairies free, and the three of you can get there faster than the rest of us." Seeing the tears welling up in Neridah's eyes, he backed away from her. "Go woman! There are innocent dinner guests at the house, they need you. I'll not be far behind."

As the Reverend turned his back on the only woman he'd ever loved, Bandah flew over and hovered in front of her. "Don't worry yourself, I'll see to it that he returns unharmed. The Trinity needs to hold together if you're to take on what's likely already passed through the portal. But you may need more than just the Trinity, so I'll send some of the pixie squadrons to help drive them back while you await our return."

"Then, can't Alfred join us now too?"

Bandah shook his head. "Should Sellemae stir, we'll need his powers as well as Colin's guns to help hold her back while we make our escape."

Neridah spoke through tears. "But, there must—"

"There isn't! Go now! Lives are at stake!"

CHAPTER 14

Heartbroken, Neridah turned away and joined hands with her kin. They allowed themselves to be back at the house and the darkness of Sellemae's chamber faded away, replaced by the familiar walls of the dining room. Patsy asked her mother, "Why didn't we need to use the portal, like before?"

"With three generations of us together, we can create an echo portal, allowing us to cross worlds some distance from the real portal's centre."

Neridah walked around the table, marvelling at the walls she'd not seen in decades. So little had changed in the years she'd been away. She ran her hands over the texture of the wallpaper, then, remembering their purpose, she asked, "Where are your guests?"

Meredith replied, "Perhaps they've gone to the kitchen. I wonder, what would our guests do in this situation?"

Patsy replied, "I'd look for a way to protect myself."

Neridah looked at Meredith and said, "She's right, that's what I'd do too."

Meredith asked, "How? With what?"

Patsy answered, "I'd go down to the shed, the one at the bottom of the garden. There's plenty of tools down there… all manner of large forks, hoes, and shovels."

Neridah walked to a window, pushing aside the curtains. "Yes, of course! Look Meredith, there… Patsy's right. Do you see the lights burning down by the shed?" Meredith and Patsy joined her by the window. "We'd better get down there, quickly."

They formed a circle, closed their eyes and held hands, allowing themselves to be elsewhere. A few seconds later, they were standing next to the shed in the pouring rain. The dinner guests were still struggling to get Vincent out from under the giant rat.

Cook looked at the three women, fear filling her eyes. "By all the saints in heaven, I ask you, what is this?" She looked at Neridah. "This cannot be! I've not seen you since I was a wee child and my mother worked for your father. You went missing decades ago! How can this be? You've not aged a day! Are you a ghost, come back to haunt us? Are Lady Meredith and Patricia ghosts too?" She backed away, crossing herself as she went. "Is that how you came to appear, as if by some form of witchcraft?"

Neridah approached Cook, hoping to ease her anxiety. "I can assure you, we are all very much alive. You have nothing to fear. Yes, we are witches, but not as you understand witches to be. We are descended from a long line of Witches of the Crossworlds. For countless centuries, our ancestors have helped maintain the natural order, protecting this world from those who would seek to do it harm. We are all that's left of the family line that once numbered in the hundreds."

Patsy said, "It's okay, Cook, there's no need to be scared. At least, not while we're around."

Charles Danbury pointed toward the distant glow that emanated from the pool, silhouetting a small army of Sellemae's minions. "Judging by the shadowy creatures coming from down there, I'd say we have a good deal to fear."

Meredith stepped forward, taking her mother and daughter by the hand. "We can create a protective shield, like we did in the chamber. It can hold them at bay and keep everyone safe until Colin and the Reverend return."

Patsy approached Mrs Bradshaw. The old widow's wet hair had fallen out of its bun and clung to her face in strands resembling rat tails. She was shivering, despite the blanket wrapped tight around her. Patsy said, "I understand that what you did before was because of the mind thief, and that you're probably not like that at all."

"Is that what you think? Huh! I've never encountered such an ill-disciplined child. I didn't need that infernal creature in my head to see the importance of teaching you some manners."

Patsy's jaw dropped. She was about to say something when Meredith put a hand on her shoulder and said, "Don't worry about her. We've far more important issues to deal with. She'll be replaced before your next lessons anyway."

The old woman stared at Meredith, her eyes conveying her utter contempt. "Good luck to you with that. I've certainly no intention of ever returning."

Meredith led Patsy away from the old widow as Bandah's pixies arrived. They took the utmost care lifting the dead rat away from Vincent, finally allowing him to get a decent breath into his lungs.

Cook ran to him once he was freed, helping the man to his feet. He was only a few years older than Cook but had kept in good shape. The pain in his chest told him he'd broken at least a few ribs. "You saved me, Cook. God love you, you saved me from that wretched spider."

Cook replied, "I'm not scared of those terrible things now." She looked across at Patsy, then back to Vincent. "I used to be, but not anymore, not while I've got a shovel and a good shoe on my foot."

Neridah addressed the pixies: "You need to hurry. You need to get to the pool and stop those things coming through. But whatever you do, don't seal the portal yet. Colin and my Alfred still have to return. Once they're back, we'll shift the portal's alignment to link with a different crossworld, so we're safe from Sellemae forever."

Charles called out, "Those things are getting closer!"

Neridah looked at Meredith and Patsy. "Okay, let's do this." The witches held hands and stood with their backs to each other while creating a fresh ball of energy, illuminating the bottom of the garden as it grew.

Neridah called out to the guests, "You must all step within the ball of light. It will keep us safe. Once it hardens, those outside will have no choice but to remain there."

The guests were hesitant at first, then Lily Danbury stepped forward. "This is all so confronting... and terrifying. But I feel there's little choice but to trust you three... and your pixies." She looked at Meredith; strong, proud, and drenched through as she stood wearing nothing but her full-length slip and jewellery. "I certainly trust you more than those other creatures. And I don't ever want to experience again what we went through earlier tonight." Her husband, Charles, took her hand and followed her.

Next to step forward were Vincent and Cook. Those remaining found themselves feeling more vulnerable being outside, particularly with the creatures of darkness getting closer.

One by one they moved into the protection of the shield… all except one.

Mrs Bradshaw stood defiantly outside the circle. "I don't trust you people. I don't trust any of you!"

Charles Danbury called out to her, "Don't be foolish, woman. Didn't you see that thing that attacked Vincent? You need to get in here now."

As Charles extended his hand to her, she backed away further. "I don't trust any form of so-called protection that relies on that petulant young girl… or any of her family for that matter."

Charles moved to the edge of the shield, arm still extended, and pleaded with her. "Don't be foolish, woman, you'll be far safer with the rest of us. If you're not prepared to come willingly, then I'll be forced to go out there and drag you in. One way or the other, it's going to happen. So, spare us all the angst and take my hand."

Mrs Bradshaw collapsed to her knees and broke down crying. "You just don't understand, do you? *I liked it!* I enjoyed the power I felt when I shared my mind with that thing. I've been one with it for years. It understood what I wanted. It wanted to help me attain all those things I'd ever…"

Charles cut her off. "Enough! I don't care how much you may wish to protest, I'm not prepared to sit here and watch those beasts take you." He left the protection of the circle, slipping and sliding his way through the mud till he reached the woman.

Mrs Bradshaw struggled to her feet, desperate to get away, only to lose her footing and fall flat on her face. "Why can't you just leave me be?"

"Because I want you to live."

The light of the shield started fading as it began to harden. The time for talk was over. Charles threw the reluctant widow over his shoulder and began the arduous and slippery few steps back to the safety of the shield.

The dwindling light of the hardening ball was still enough to illuminate a giant bat swooping down on Charles before he was even halfway there. He dived forward, sliding to a stop just short of his goal. A pair of shadows swept through them. Charles immediately recognised the mind thief for what it was, focusing hard to shut it out, and determined not to be taken over again.

Mrs Bradshaw was a different story. She welcomed the mind thief with open arms. Once fully under its control, she burst out laughing, then said, "Oh please, save me, Charles! Let me tear you all apart from within the safety of your fragile little shell. One way or the other, you will all die to—"

Charles put a hand over her mouth and pulled her to the ground. He dragged her with him as he pushed into the glowing light of the shield. Although it felt like walking through a sea of molasses, he was still able to struggle through its outer layers till Vincent reached out and grabbed Mrs Bradshaw from him, dragging her through just before the shield had sealed. Charles felt the hardening energy push him back until he collapsed to the ground exhausted.

He was shut out.

Inside the shield, Mrs Bradshaw lunged at the witches. The guests responded quickly, bringing her to the ground and holding her there. Madness filled her eyes as she screamed, "Fools! You'll wish you were dead by sunrise!"

Meanwhile, outside the shield, Charles raised his head from the mud just in time to see a bat preparing to grab him by his shoulders. Patsy felt his distress as the claws sank into his flesh and lifted him off the ground.

A sound like a crack of thunder echoed and the bat fell to the ground, releasing its cargo.

Colin McIntyre was pleased that his marksmanship hadn't let him down.

Patsy couldn't contain her excitement. "Father's made it back!"

Meredith expelled a sigh of relief, while Neridah anxiously waited for some sign of Alfred's return.

Dozens of giant bats and rats crashed into the shield with each passing second, bouncing back with serious burns where they'd made impact. Charles lay on the ground, attempting to be as still as he could in an effort to avoid attracting attention. But it was no good. The rogue fairy who'd ridden the now dead rat approached him. "It took me years to tame that bat. You'll pay for this, pitiful human scum."

Patsy turned to Neridah and Meredith. "I need to rescue him."

Her mother shook her head. "You can't. It's too great a risk."

Neridah disagreed. "Hush, Meredith! Listen to her... there's a man who needs saving, and we must do what we can. It's been our duty for countless generations. You and I can hold this barrier for at least the few seconds it will take for her to help him."

Meredith protested, "It should be one of us! She's just a child... my child."

"She's also my grandchild, and the most powerful one among us, by a long way. Neither you nor I would have as good a chance of success as she will." Neridah glanced down at Patsy. "Go on, do as you must, bring him to safety."

Patsy allowed herself to be outside the shield, standing next to Charles Danbury. She stared at the rogue. "You should know by now. I'm not scared of fairies."

The rogue sneered and drew back her wand. "Well, you should be."

"You don't want to know what happened to the last fairy who said that to me." A frown grew across Patsy's brow as she stomped her foot. A reverberation ran through the ground, throwing the rogue off balance.

The rogue brought her arm forward, aiming the wand toward Patsy. But the girl was too quick, sending forth a small surge of energy that knocked the fairy to the ground. Patsy wrapped her arms around Charles's shoulders.

"Don't worry Mister Danbury, if you can just empty your mind, I can take you to safety."

He looked across at Mrs Bradshaw, struggling against the guests holding her down. "But, if I empty my mind, won't I be vulnerable too?"

"Mister Danbury, you may think of me as little more than a child, but you must know by now that I'm more than that. I promise, I will get you to safety."

Charles looked into her eyes, convinced by her confidence that his best option was to trust her.

He closed his eyes.

When he opened them a second later, they were inside the fast-shrinking shield.

Meredith called to her, "Quickly, Patricia… we can't hold this any longer without you."

Realising every second mattered, Patsy allowed herself to be standing with her mother and grandmother, saving the time it would have taken to walk the few steps otherwise. Meredith was speechless. She'd couldn't believe how much confidence her daughter was developing in her capabilities… capabilities she'd known nothing of just twelve hours earlier. "You've mastered the craft more tonight than I have in my entire life."

Neridah smiled and added, "Perhaps she's felt more reason in this one night than you had throughout your life. I'm guessing that you've mastered your skills more tonight than throughout the rest of your life as well."

"Yes, that's true. I've never looked to do much more than listen to nature. After your disappearance, and Grandfather's passing, my grandmother had little appetite to teach me the craft. But it didn't matter, I don't think I ever had the appetite for such things anyway."

"Oh, Meredith, my darling daughter. You've grown to be such a strong-minded woman, and I believe you to be a far more powerful witch than you realise. It's because of who you are that Patricia is so powerful."

The sound of further gunshots drew their focus back to the battle. Meredith watched the constant flow of beasts bouncing off their shield. "We can't hold this in place forever, and I fear there's too many beasts for Colin and the Reverend to deal with, even with Bandah and his pixies helping them. One of us needs to go out and join them, or these creatures will wear us down. Mother, you and Patsy are strong together. I'll go and you two can hold the shield in place."

Neridah broke away from the circle. "No! It has to be me."

Meredith was horrified. "Mother! No, you can't!"

Neridah replied, "There's no other way. Patricia is stronger than both you and I together. If you maintain focus, her strength is enough that the two of you can hold the shield. You're her mother." She looked down at Patsy. "She'll need you more than she'll need me." Turning back to Meredith, she continued, "If I don't make it back, I'll have gone down fighting for what I believe in." In the next instant, Neridah was gone.

Meredith was dumbstruck. She spoke to the empty space where her mother had been. "You'd better make it back here! If you don't, we're doomed!"

•

The pool was unrecognisable, the water now a spinning vortex with a hollow centre. Where its bottom had been there was now an open portal to darkness.

More creatures came through. It had become akin to a magnet within the Spider Queen's realm, sucking creatures in like a strong rip current at a surf beach.

Having freed the fairies in Sellemae's choir, Colin and the Reverend couldn't escape being caught up in the surge.

As they were swept along, the Reverend had a word with Bandah. "You need to stop them using the portal once we've passed through. There must already be hundreds of these vermin on the other side by now."

"We'll make a net with the silk from Sellemae's cocoons. As well as stopping more going through, it can catch anything you may be able to send back from the other side."

"Will that not take time to weave?"

"You underestimate what a few thousand pixies can achieve working together."

Colin asked, "How will you get back when we've closed the portal from the other side?"

Bandah laughed. "We'll be fine. Pixies don't need portals to travel between crossworlds. Now go, you've no time for idle banter, the witches will need your help."

The Reverend and Colin were drawn toward the portal, side by side with the creatures of darkness, swinging their blades from time to time when the turbulence brought them close enough to strike at their foes.

They lost control of their movements as they were sucked through the portal, the force sending them flying into the bushes near the creek, as though they'd been flung by a catapult.

On getting his breath back, Colin reloaded his revolver and flintlock while the Reverend slashed with his sword at anything that came close. Seeing the pixies poking and prodding the creatures that had already made it through (like a hive of hornets attacking a herd of animals), the Reverend said, "I'm glad to see the pixies doing what they can to slow the beasts down."

Colin replied, "Yes, but they're greatly outnumbered, and hitting pressure points does little more than buy us time."

The Reverend looked up toward the garden shed. "Aye, that may be the case, but can you see the glow? Your family are protecting the guests and themselves with a shield."

Colin stood on a rock to gain a better view. "Yes, I can see that, but look, there's someone outside the shield. It looks like Charles, and there's a bat bearing down on him!" Colin raised the flintlock to his shoulder and fired, bringing the beast to the ground. "We need to provide some cover if we want to give Meredith and the others a chance to get him in."

"There's not much I can do from this distance. If I try to send anything that far, it'll almost certainly lose most of its power by the time it gets there."

"Then we need to get closer."

The two men ran forward with scant regard for their safety. As they ran, the Reverend noticed the flow of creatures coming through the portal had stopped. "Bandah's been as good as his word. Time to send some of these foul beasts back from whence they came." He stretched his arm toward the bat closest to the portal and flung his hand downwards. It was as though an invisible rope connecting his arm with the beast had sent both bat and rider hurtling back toward the portal.

Colin called out, "I'll take out the biggest." He continued running as he fired his revolver, each shot hitting its mark with his usual accuracy.

The Reverend's pace slowed as he continued throwing the creatures back to the portal. Those who'd been stunned by the pixies hitting their pressure points were the easiest targets, but there were still hundreds more to be dealt with. "We've no chance if we continue this way. We need to use more facets of the craft than I'm versed in if we're to send all these vermin back to their foul home."

As if on cue, Neridah appeared next to him. She took his hands and drew him in close. "Alfred! Thank God, you made it back!"

"Aye, that we did. But it'll be for naught if we don't do something to drive these beasts back."

She took his hands in hers. "Do you trust me?"

"I'd not have dedicated my life to crossing between the worlds to get you back if there were any doubt of that."

"Then hold my hands, do as I do." Neridah began reciting a mantra: "Tishbah reign de nigh, tishbah reign de nigh…"

The Reverend joined in and their eyes locked on each other, as though they were boring into each other's souls. Their feet started rising and they drifted as far away from each other as their extended arms would allow.

As they rose further, the two of them appeared to be lying on their bellies in mid-air. Then, they started to spin. Very slowly at first, but picking up speed as they went. Realising what they were up to, the creatures of darkness turned their attention away from the shield and the house guests.

The pixies formed themselves into a barrier surrounding Neridah and the Reverend, immobilising any who came near.

The pair rose and drifted till they were spinning directly above the portal, their arms pulling hard against each other from the centrifugal force.

With the spell in full flight, there was no longer any need for them to continue the mantra.

Their strategy seemed to be working. The creatures who'd come through the portal were now being drawn back to it.

Unfortunately, that included Colin.

When he felt himself starting to be sucked toward the portal, he grabbed hold of a nearby tree with a trunk that was almost half a metre in diameter. He put his flintlock on the far side of the tree and grabbed hold of it from either end just as the wind rushing toward the portal lifted his feet from the ground. Once satisfied that his grip was strong enough to hold him, he looked up and watched as the creatures of darkness were sucked into the portal.

Neridah looked at the Reverend. "I don't think I can hold on for much longer... my hands... they're slipping." The Reverend tightened his grip as much as possible, but he could tell she was right. It was not a matter of if she'd slip from his grasp, but when. Neridah continued, "When I let go, the portal will snap shut, and whatever's left here shall remain."

The beasts tried to resist the force of the spell drawing them to the portal, but it was to no avail. Dozens were hurtling in, the pace increasing as Neridah and the Reverend spun faster and faster.

Colin's grip on the flintlock was slipping too. He began worrying that it may come apart under the force, throwing him back into the Spider Queen's realm.

Eventually, his fingers had slipped too far, and he went hurtling toward the darkness at the pool's centre.

Neridah's grip failed as well, causing her and the Reverend to fall, crashing to the pool below as the portal snapped shut, with Colin right at its outer edge. A tenth of a second longer, and he would have been gone.

Neridah and the Reverend stood up, their clothing weighing them down in the metre-deep water. Hand in hand, they made their way to the shore in silence. For now, their powers were exhausted. It would be up to Meredith, Patsy and the pixies to deal with the remaining creatures of darkness.

Colin watched them approach the shore as he reloaded his gun. He called out as loud as he could, hoping to be heard over the rain, "Did you notice how many are left?"

The Reverend shook his head. "My guess is there's likely at least fifty."

A flash of lightning revealed a giant spider preparing to bite down on Colin's shoulder. The Reverend, too exhausted to use his power, and no longer in possession of his sword (it had been stripped from him by the centrifugal force), reached for his boot where he kept a small blade. In one fluid action, he brought it to the surface and sent it flying through the air. Colin felt it whistle past his ear before it found its mark. The spider was wounded, but not enough for it to give up. Colin, having finished reloading his revolver, fired just before the spider's fangs could pierce his flesh.

No sooner had the spider fallen than a rat leapt from the bushes. Colin fired two more shots, causing the creature to let out a blood-curdling squeal as it came down on top of him, knocking the revolver from his hand. A rogue fairy climbed off the rodent's back and laughed as she drew back her wand. "Well, this should be easy. I'll end your misery, then drag those two fools back to face their fate at the hands of Sellemae."

A flash of light, brighter than anything they'd seen that night, was accompanied by a deafening crack of thunder. The ground moved as if being carried on a wave. Trees were uprooted, and giant boulders went flying. The rogue stood frozen as she realised the origin of the earth tremor. There, at the central point from which the wave had come, stood Patsy, the upheaval having been the result of her stomping her foot in anger. "Leave my father alone!"

The rogue grinned, then turned to Colin. "Prepare to die, you useless waste of breath and flesh."

The rogue was pushed hard against a nearby tree. Then Patsy lifted her finger and the rogue flew into the air, completely at her mercy. She pointed toward the centre of the pool, sending the rogue toward a miniature portal she'd opened with barely a thought. Once the first rogue had been dispatched, she began flinging her arms about, each movement capturing several creatures of darkness that she then threw back into Sellemae's world. When the last of the creatures had been expelled, Patsy collapsed and blacked out, utterly exhausted.

Colin ran to his daughter while the Reverend and Neridah dragged themselves from the pool as its waters swept in to fill the void the closing portal had created.

A noise from the centre of the pool drew the Reverend's attention. It was Sellemae! One of her fang-tipped limbs was rising above the water, followed a moment later by another.

Meredith had already started to run down the hill to be with Patsy. When she saw the Spider Queen's legs coming through, she knew it was up to her, and her alone.

She had to end this.

While the pixies could possibly buy her time, she was the only one there who could potentially shut the portal that Sellemae held open. She drew her arms back and took a deep breath, focusing everything she had on drawing strings of energy from as many of the crossworlds as possible. She felt immense power surge through her, making her glow like the sun. She drew so much energy that bringing her hands down by her side triggered a flash of lightning and a crack of thunder, along with another wave that moved earth, rocks and trees, just like her daughter.

When the power surge reached the centre of the pool, Sellemae's limbs disintegrated, leaving behind droplets of water that fell harmlessly back to the pool with the rest of the rain.

The portal to Sellemae's world was finally closed, once and for all.

Meredith swayed on the spot for a few seconds before her knees gave way and she fell to the ground.

Three generations of witches and the Reverend Casey were all passed out. Colin slumped his back against a tree, then looked up and opened his mouth in the hope of catching some rain.

It took a while for him to register the voice calling out to him. It wasn't until it was almost directly next to him that he bothered to turn and pay attention to where it came from. There was Cook, full of concern, Vincent by her side. Cook asked, "Mister McIntyre! Are you alright, sir?"

"Yes, Cook, I don't know how, but I believe I am."

"Oh, but begging your pardon, sir, we still have the problem of Mrs Bradshaw. It's taking eight people to hold her down, and they're all getting frightfully tired, sir."

A mind thief! At least there was just the one to deal with. "Vincent, may I ask a favour?" He didn't wait for a response before continuing. "Be a good man and grab some rope from the shed to tie her up until we're all indoors and dried off. We'll need Bandah's help with this. Everyone else with powers seems to be taking a well-earned rest."

Vincent nodded and headed off to the shed while Cook helped Colin to his feet.

Colin told her, "He's a good man you know, never married either."

"Now don't you go getting any harebrained ideas in your head, Mister McIntyre."

Colin surprised himself by smiling and somehow finding the energy to let out a whole-hearted laugh. He thought to himself that sometimes, good things were indeed born out of the bad.

Colin and Cook worked their way up the hill, while the pixies banded together to transport the three unconscious witches and the Reverend to the house. The rain was easing, and the first light of dawn was visible as the guests carried the tied up, and struggling, Mrs Bradshaw.

Once at the house, Bandah instructed the guests to place her on the kitchen table. A hundred pixies gathered around her and began pushing their hands in and under the surface of her flesh, like people searching with their hands for an object in muddy water. Eventually, one of them called out, "I've found it!" He pulled his hand out, revealing part of a shadow. The rest of the pixies joined him, tugging and pulling at the shadow until it was fully out.

Mrs Bradshaw then fell into a deep sleep.

The mind thief, feeling vulnerable and outnumbered, disappeared into another crossworld.

Lily Danbury asked Bandah, "Will it be back?"

"Oh yes, but not in this household. Mind thieves come and go in your world all the time. They like to target politicians and kings, even business leaders. There is more of what you might call magic, good and bad, happening around you every day than you're aware of."

*

A day later, the dinner guests were in good spirits. None of them had any memory of what had taken place, just that their weekend had been somehow extraordinary. They were grateful that Colin had sent stable hands to retrieve their horses that had escaped in the Friday night storm.

Mrs Bradshaw's driver had no idea what the injury had been that led to the bandage wrapped around his head. All he knew was that he had a frightful headache as a result.

As Mrs Bradshaw climbed into the carriage, she said, "Driver, take me away from this wretched place." Once seated, she looked out the window at Meredith and declared, "You need to find yourself another tutor. The idea that I should spend any more time with that petulant child is incomprehensible."

Meredith replied, "I'm glad there's something we can agree on." The driver cracked his whip and the carriage took off.

Vincent approached Cook. "I'll be heading down to Sydney next week to listen to the opera. Would you care to join me? That is, if Mister McIntyre is agreeable to you having the time off work." Cook looked up at Colin and his smile told her everything she needed to know. Vincent climbed onto his horse, tipped his hat at Cook, and rode off.

Neridah walked with the Reverend Alfred Casey to his sulky. "So, you chose to be a man of the cloth?"

Alfred responded with a silent nod.

"Are you sure you have to go?"

"Aye, but I promise you, I'll be back… soon."

As they walked, Neridah grabbed his arm and made sure she had eye contact. "I never knew how powerful a thing love can be. Your whole life, devoted to an impossible dream of bringing me back."

"A dream that has finally come true."

She stopped walking and took his hands in hers. "If you want me, Alfred, I'm yours, and I always will be, whatever may happen."

"I know." Alfred gave Neridah one last hug, then climbed onto his sulky and rode away without another word.

.

Down by the pool, Meredith and Patsy sat listening to the rescued fairies sing joyful songs celebrating their freedom.

As one song finished and another began, Patsy turned her focus to stroking Ferdinand's back as the cat lay purring on her lap. "Tell me what you really think, Mother. Can we trust these ones?"

Meredith looked at her and smiled. "They'll be fine."

The cat stuck his head up to offer his opinion. "You would hope so. After all, you did save them from an eternity of suffering."

But there was one rescued fairy who wasn't singing, and that fairy was Mrs Smith.

She looked dejected as she sat on a nearby bough, well away from the other fairies. Glaring at the witches she grumbled, "Ha! Why would I be grateful? I'd have been happier if you'd left me behind to sing in Sellemae's chamber."

Meredith gave a puzzled look. "Really? I'm curious why you feel that way, Mrs Smith."

Patsy looked the fairy in the eye. "Yes, come on, Mrs Smith, how about some gratitude. After all, you don't want to make me angry, do you?" Patsy tried her best to look serious, but broke out giggling as the pretence faded.

The laughter came to an abrupt halt when Patsy noticed a glow emanating from the centre of the pool. Ripples of water bounced around and a creature Patsy hadn't seen the like of came through the portal.

In a way, it appeared similar to the other fairies, but then she noticed the distinct lack of substance. It seemed almost as though the creature was half in this world and half in another.

It flew towards Patsy and whispered, "She is coming."

A moment later, the creature was gone.

THE STORY CONTINUES IN

The Witches of the Crossworlds: Hunter

www.ingramcontent.com/pod-product-compliance
Lightning Source LLC
Chambersburg PA
CBHW020529120726
47904CB00003B/1010